WITCHES' CAT

WITCHES AND WINE BOOK 7

MORGANA BEST

BEST
Cosy Books

GLOSSARY

*S*ome Australian spellings and expressions are entirely different from US spellings and expressions. Below are just a few examples. It would take an entire book to list all the differences.

The author has used Australian spelling in this series. Here are a few examples: *Mum* instead of the US spelling *Mom*, *neighbour* instead of the US spelling *neighbor*, *realise* instead of the US spelling *realize*. It is *Ms*, *Mr* and *Mrs* in Australia, not *Ms.*, *Mr.* and *Mrs.*; *defence* not *defense*; *judgement* not *judgment*; *cosy* and not *cozy*; *1930s* not *1930's*; *offence* not *offense*; *centre* not *center*; *towards* not *toward*; *jewellery* not *jewelry*; *favour* not *favor*; *mould* not *mold*; *two storey house* not *two story house*; *practise* (verb) not *practice* (verb); *odour* not *odor*; *smelt* not *smelled*; *travelling* not *traveling*; *liquorice* not *licorice*; *cheque* not *check*; *leant* not *leaned*; *have concussion* not *have a concussion*; *anti clockwise* not *counterclockwise*; *go to hospital* not *go to the hospital*; *sceptic* not *skeptic*; *aluminium* not *aluminum*; *learnt* not *learned*. We have *fancy dress* parties not *costume* parties. We don't say *gotten*. We say *car crash* (or *accident*) not *car wreck*. We say *a herb* not *an herb* as we pronounce the 'h.'

The above are just a few examples.

It's not just different words; Aussies sometimes use different expressions in sentence structure. We might *eat a curry* not *eat curry*. We might say *in the main street* not *on the main street*. Someone might be *going well* instead of *doing well*. We might say *without drawing breath* not *without drawing a breath*.

These are just some of the differences.

Please note that these are not mistakes or typos, but correct, normal Aussie spelling, terms, and syntax.

AUSTRALIAN SLANG AND TERMS

Benchtops - counter tops (kitchen)
Big Smoke - a city

Blighter - infuriating or good-for-nothing person

Blimey! - an expression of surprise

Bloke - a man (usually used in nice sense, "a good bloke")

Blue (noun) - an argument ("to have a blue")

Bluestone - copper sulphate (copper sulfate in US spelling)

Bluo - a blue laundry additive, an optical brightener

Boot (car) - trunk (car)

Bonnet (car) - hood (car)

Bore - a drilled water well

Budgie smugglers (variant: budgy smugglers) - named after the Aussie native bird, the budgerigar. A slang term for brief and tight-fitting men's swimwear

Bugger! - as an expression of surprise, not a swear word

Bugger - as in "the poor bugger" - refers to an unfortunate person (not a swear word)

Bunging it on - faking something, pretending

Bush telegraph - the grapevine, the way news spreads by word of mouth in the country

Car park - parking lot

Cark it - die

Chooks - chickens

Come good - turn out okay

Copper, cop - police officer

Coot - silly or annoying person

Cream bun - a sweet bread roll with copious amounts of cream, plus jam (= jelly in US) in the centre

Crook - 1. "Go crook (on someone)" - to berate them. 2. (someone is) crook - (someone is) ill. 3.

Crook (noun) - a criminal

Demister (in car) - defroster

Drongo - an idiot

Dunny - an outhouse, a toilet, often ramshackle

Fair crack of the whip - a request to be fair, reasonable, just

Flannelette (fabric) - cotton, wool, or synthetic fabric, one side of which has a soft finish.

Flat out like a lizard drinking water - very busy

Galah - an idiot

Garbage - trash

G'day - Hello

Give a lift (to someone) - give a ride (to someone)

Goosebumps - goose pimples

Gumboots - rubber boots, wellingtons

Knickers - women's underwear

Laundry (referring to the room) - laundry room

Lamingtons - iconic Aussie cakes, square, sponge, chocolate-dipped, and coated with desiccated coconut. Some have a layer of cream and strawberry jam (= jelly in US) between the two halves.

Lift - elevator

Like a stunned mullet - very surprised

Mad as a cut snake - either insane or very angry

Mallee bull (as fit as, as mad as) - angry and/or fit, robust, super strong.

Miles - while Australians have kilometres these days, it is common to use expressions such as, "The road stretched for miles," "It was miles away."

Moleskins - woven heavy cotton fabric with suede-like finish, commonly used as working wear, or as town clothes

Mow (grass / lawn) - cut (grass / lawn)

Neenish tarts - Aussie tart. Pastry base. Filling is based on sweetened condensed milk mixture or mock cream. Some have layer of raspberry jam (jam = jelly in US). Topping is in two equal halves: icing (= frosting in US), usually chocolate on one side, and either lemon or pink or the other.

Pub - The pub at the south of a small town is often referred to as the 'bottom pub' and the pub at the north end of town, the 'top pub.' The size of a small town is often judged by the number of pubs - i.e. "It's a three pub town."

Red cattle dog - (variant: blue cattle dog usually known as a 'blue dog') - referring to the breed of Australian Cattle Dog. However, a 'red dog' is usually a red kelpie (another breed of dog)

Shoot through - leave

Shout (a drink) - to buy a drink for someone

Skull (a drink) - drink a whole drink without stopping

Stone the crows! - an expression of surprise

Takeaway (food) - Take Out (food)

Toilet - also refers to the room if it is separate from the bathroom

Torch - flashlight

Tuck in (to food) - to eat food hungrily

Ute /Utility - pickup truck

Vegemite - Australian food spread, thick, dark brown

Wardrobe - closet

Windscreen - windshield

Indigenous References

Bush tucker - food that occurs in the Australian bush

Koori - the original inhabitants/traditional custodians of the land of Australia in the part of NSW in which this book is set. *Murri* are the people just to the north. White European culture often uses the term, *Aboriginal people*.

CHAPTER 1

"*H*is name is Cary," Aunt Maude said as she held up the small Dachshund. "After Cary Grant."

Aunt Agnes, Aunt Dorothy, and I exchanged glances, but Maude did not seem to notice. She was too taken with Cary, who was nuzzling her with his damp little nose.

"He's a sausage dog," I said, confused. I wondered what Breena, the shifter cat, would think of him. I opened my mouth to voice my concern, but Agnes and Maude shook their heads.

"A sausage dog named Cary," Maude repeated. "He's a rescue. I just bought him from the shelter."

"We can talk about Maude's new dog later,

Valkyrie," Aunt Maude whispered. "Maude has a date tonight."

"I have a date too," I replied, "with Lucas. I'm going to head to my cottage to check my make-up again."

Maude shook her head. "You can't go just yet. You have to stay with my sisters and see if this man is suitable. He's quite a bit younger than I am."

"How much younger?"

"He's eighty-five."

"Straight out of college then," I said, which earned me a jab in the ribs from Agnes's elbow. "What's the guy's name, and is he allergic to dogs, seeing as we apparently have a dog now?"

"His name is Pillsbury," Maude said, and she blushed a little. "He's—well, he still has all his hair."

"So does my date," I said as I tried to step from the room.

Agnes blocked my exit. "Valkyrie, please stay to give your opinion on Maude's date."

"He's coming here," Maude replied.

"Don't tell me we have two new rescues instead of one."

"He's staying for dinner, Valkyrie. Not forever."

"Of course, I support you, Aunt Maude. I just

wish I could support you tomorrow. I don't have much time left with Lucas until he needs to leave the country."

"You don't have to stay the whole time, Valkyrie, just long enough to give me your impression."

So the aunts stood by the living room window, waiting for Pillsbury to appear. Cary lay on the antique chaise, dreaming his little Dachshund dreams. He didn't even stir when Pillsbury's car pulled up, and a little old man sprang from the driver's seat, dressed in a suit that was perhaps popular in the seventies. He was wearing bell-bottoms and all.

I watched with growing intrigue as Pillsbury skipped down the driveway, a bouquet of daisies held firm in his right hand. With his left hand, he rang the doorbell.

Maude hissed at us to get away from the window. "Wait until I'm upstairs," she instructed, "and then open the door."

"But he's your date," Dorothy protested. "Don't you want to say hello?"

"I will say hello, but only after I have descended the stairs like an elegant woman."

Rolling her eyes, Dorothy waited for Maude to

scurry up the stairs, and then she opened the door. "Hello, you must be Pillsbury. Maude is expecting you. My name is Dorothy."

"Enchanted," Pillsbury said, and he kissed Dorothy's hand.

Agnes stepped forward. "I'm Agnes. Maude is our sister. And this is Valkyrie, our niece."

"Surely neither of you are old enough to have a grown-up niece," Pillsbury said.

Agnes and Dorothy giggled. I did my best not to groan.

I was getting ready to make my escape, but Pillsbury and Agnes pulled me into the kitchen. It turned out that Pillsbury and Maude planned to have their date at home, and as Pillsbury was going to cook for her, he needed help in the kitchen. He put a link of sausages on the kitchen counter.

"You ladies wouldn't happen to have any alcohol, would you?" Pillsbury said, looking at us hopefully. "I don't mean wine; I mean alcohol to start fires. I spent a lot of years as a stockman, so I'm more used to cooking over a campfire."

"Err, not really," I replied, confused. "I think we do have some rubbing alcohol." I looked under the kitchen sink and found some.

Pillsbury nodded happily. "Perfect. Hand me the bottle."

With a swoop of fear in my stomach, I handed Pillsbury the bottle of rubbing alcohol. I stood back as Pillsbury put one of the sausages on a plate, dosed it in rubbing alcohol, and set it on fire.

It was at this time Dorothy entered the room, still not wearing her glasses, asking if anyone had seen the sausage dog, Cary, who seemed to have disappeared. She took one look at the sausage engulfed with flames and started to scream.

"It's just a sausage, Aunt Dorothy," I said.

"His name," Dorothy replied, "is Cary!"

She threw herself onto the kitchen counter, putting out the flames with her rather large bosom, which then caught fire. Pillsbury managed to put out these flames with his hands, which gave Maude quite a big shock when she walked into the kitchen.

"The fire was too large to ignore," Pillsbury said to Maude, who raised an eyebrow.

"Yes, I am well acquainted with temptation, Pillsbury. I was once young myself, you know. But cheating on me before we are even together with my sister and in front of our niece is an absolutely horrific thing to do."

"Aunt Maude," I said then, "you've got Cary."

Indeed, the sausage dog was snuggled up in Maude's arms, wagging his little tail. "Yes," Maude replied, "I took him outside so he could do his business with some dignity. Not that any of you would know about dignity."

"Pillsbury set fire to his sausage," Dorothy snapped. She did not know how to explain herself well, and she seemed offended that Maude could ever imagine she would make a move on one of her sister's gentlemen callers.

"That is quite enough of that," Pillsbury cried softly. "There is nothing wrong with my sausage."

"Oh, for goodness' sake!" I exclaimed. "Dorothy was not wearing her glasses and thought Pillsbury had set fire to Cary. She threw herself onto the sausage, putting out the fire with her bosom. Her bosom then caught on fire, and Pillsbury had to put it out with hands. See, there is a perfectly reasonable explanation for this madness."

"*Perfectly reasonable* are not the words I would use," Maude said as she placed Cary on the ground. He didn't seem the least bit interested in the drama.

I dusted my hands. "Right. I have a hot date with Lucas. Goodbye."

I hurried back to the cottage as the smell of burnt sausage was clinging to my silk dress. I would have to change now after Pillsbury's little act with the sausage and the rubbing alcohol. Where did my aunts find these men? Actually, I did not want to know.

I slipped out of my dress before rummaging through the pile of laundry on my floor. It was clean laundry, pulled off my bed the night before because I could not be bothered sorting and folding and putting everything away. I tied on a halter-top dress, the kind which was popular in the nineties and was popular again now, and ran to the front door when I heard the knock.

It was Lucas. He was tall, dark, and late. "Did you try to cook me dinner?"

"Pillsbury set fire to his sausage."

"Do I even want to know what that means?"

I laughed. "It means exactly what it says on the tin. Are we ready to go?"

"Don't you want to grab a jacket?" Lucas said. He was wearing a black jacket, and I thought he looked very dashing indeed.

"If I wear a jacket, then I can't wear your jacket."

"Are you going to wear my jacket?"

"Of course," I said, "because I am going to pretend I am very cold."

"Fair enough." Lucas placed his jacket over my shoulders now, perhaps to save time, and he led me with a firm hand on my back to his car.

It didn't take long for us to arrive at the restaurant, which was part of a lighthouse on a cliff. Because the lighthouse only had so much room, the restaurant was booked weeks in advance. I wondered how Lucas had even managed to wrangle a reservation, as the lighthouse restaurant was exclusive.

We ordered our main meals. Lucas wanted a sand crab lasagne, which consisted of local sand crab finished with seafood bisque, while I ordered Pad Thai with peanuts and basil.

Lucas was clearly excited to bring me here on such a romantic date. "Should we pretend I don't have to leave?" Lucas said in hushed tones before taking a sip of wine.

"Let's pretend you don't have to leave," I said, "just for a little bit, at least. Should I tell you about the Dachshund disaster I experienced tonight? Maude is currently on a terrible first date."

"I love terrible first date stories," Lucas said. "I have about a million. What about you?"

"All forgotten now," I said, and I felt a swoop of

utter delight. I would never have to go on another tragic first date again.

After dinner, Lucas ordered the fruit plate for two. That was literally its name: The Fruit Plate For Two. I remembered all those years when I would see couples looking beautiful and sweet in a restaurant and fell a pang of jealousy that I was alone. Well, I wasn't alone now. I had Lucas.

I took his hand. "I know you have to go, but I'm going to miss you."

I wanted Lucas to take me into his arms and say, "Of course, I am not going anywhere. Where you are is the only place I want to be." But he wouldn't say that because Lucas had an important mission, a mission that I needed him to undertake. He had to escort my parents to safety. I had said my goodbyes to them only hours earlier.

After lunch, we returned to his cottage at Mugwort Manor, where Lucas finished packing his suitcase. I wanted to pack for him, but that was something a wife did, and I was not his wife. So, I sprawled on the coach and stress-ate his Tim Tams as he searched for that shirt and those jeans and just where had all his socks gone? I did a good job of not helping him look. *Helping men emasculates them*, Aunt Dorothy liked to say. I didn't know if I believed this. I did know, however, that sprawling on the couch eating chocolate Tim Tams was way more fun than rummaging through a cupboard for a missing sock.

"I'll just go sockless," Lucas finally muttered.

"How naughty," I replied. "If you were an olden day genteel lady, they would burn you as a witch."

I escorted Lucas to the manor. Agnes and Dorothy were conspicuous by their absence, no doubt in order to give us some alone time. I had no idea where Maude and Pillsbury were. We slipped in the back door and headed for the secret room.

Lucas turned to say goodbye. He kissed me once on the forehead, then once on the tip of my nose, and then once more on my lips. Then he was gone, vanishing off into the gloom of the tunnel.

I waited for a while, and then turned away, sad. I would miss my parents and I would miss Lucas. I needed some cheering up, so went in search of my aunts and found them in the vegetable garden.

Before I could speak, Aunt Maude groaned. "Don't look now—it's Euphemia Jones."

We all turned to look.

"I said not to look!" Maude complained.

The unpleasant woman stomped over to us,

giving a good impression of a troll. She shook her meaty fist in my face. "You've given me food poisoning!" she exclaimed, clutching her stomach with her other hand. "I'm horribly ill and I have the most terrible stomach pains. I don't know how I was able to walk here from my cottage!"

I wiped my hand across my forehead. "Food poisoning? What do you mean?"

"It must have been the cereal," she began, but then she fell down dead.

CHAPTER 2

*A*unt Agnes let out a bloodcurdling scream. "It's Gorgona!"

Aunt Agnes and Aunt Maude bent over the victim. Aunt Dorothy was staring fixedly at the body's sturdy leather shoes as Cary chewed on a shoelace. "It looks like Euphemia Jones."

"I had no idea she was Gorgona, and she's been here renting the cottage all this time," Agnes said.

I stared at the woman's face. "But, but she's changed her appearance!" I stammered. "I am going mad? I thought it was Euphemia Jones, but it's an entirely different woman."

Aunt Agnes clutched my arm and looked around. "This is a terrible situation. What are we going to do?"

"Can somebody tell me what's going on? Was Euphemia Jones a shifter?" I cleared my throat and added, "Can people shift from one human form to another?"

"Not as such, not the way you mean it. No, when she appeared as Euphemia, it was a glamour," Aunt Agnes said.

Dorothy made a snort of disapproval. "And falling on the tomatoes, of all things. Why, they're completely squashed! It took weeks to grow the vines to that height."

I ignored her and asked, "What's a glamour?"

Aunt Agnes stomped her foot. "A glamour is a magical disguise that makes someone look like someone else. Gorgona has been here spying on us and pretending she was a woman by the name of Euphemia Jones."

I was thoroughly confused. "Shouldn't we call an ambulance? What if she's not dead?"

Aunt Agnes folded her arms over her chest. "Of course, she's dead. When somebody's wearing a vampire glamour, it disappears when they die."

"But we'll have to call the police," I said.

Maude agreed. "Yes, but we'll have to make her look like Euphemia again first."

This was getting stranger by the minute. Just

then, Breena appeared in human form, albeit with a field mouse dangling by its tail from her mouth.

"Put down that mouse," I said to her.

She ignored me and walked past Euphemia, hissing at Cary as she did. When she saw Euphemia's face, she screamed. The mouse fell from her mouth and ran away. Breena ran over to the nearest tree and shimmied up it.

I was beginning to wonder if I was having a dream—a bad dream. A *very* bad dream. None of this was making any sense. I noticed Aunt Maude was suddenly missing. "Is she calling the police?" I asked Aunt Agnes.

"She's going to get a reversing potion to make Gorgona look like Euphemia Jones again. Then we'll call the police, and while we're waiting for them to arrive, I'll explain everything."

"I hope you *do* explain everything," I said. "I don't like being kept in the dark about everything, like I usually am."

Aunt Agnes ignored my pointed remark and tried to coax Breena down from the tree, to no avail. It seemed like ages before Aunt Maude reappeared with the potion. "What took you so long?" Aunt Dorothy asked her.

"It was in the altar room at the back of a

cupboard," she said. "We haven't needed any for years, decades even. Maybe centuries." Without further words, she poured the potion all over Euphemia's face. Her face at once changed back to the original form. Okay, maybe it wasn't the original form, but it was the form in which I had always seen her.

Aunt Agnes pulled her phone out of her pocket and called the police. "This is Agnes Jasper from Mugwort Manor Bed and Breakfast. One of our clients complained of stomach pains and has fallen down dead." Aunt Agnes nodded and then added, "She's definitely dead."

"I wonder who poisoned her?" Aunt Dorothy asked, clutching Cary in her arms.

I expected Aunt Agnes to rebuke Dorothy for being so silly and fanciful, so I was surprised when she agreed with her diagnosis. "It was obviously The Other."

"The Other?" I shrieked. "Why would they want to kill that dreadful woman? I don't understand any of it. It doesn't make any sense at all."

The Other was an evil, covert group formed centuries ago to stand in direct opposition to the Council, the governing body of vampires worldwide. The Other wanted to wipe shifters off the face of the earth. My parents were currently in hiding from The Other.

"Euphemia Jones was here to spy on us," Aunt Agnes told me. "She was actually our cousin."

My hand went to my throat. "Your cousin?" I exclaimed. "She was your cousin? Then why aren't you upset?"

Aunt Agnes was trembling. "Of course, we're upset. It's a terrible shock, but you have to understand, she was estranged from us for years."

"Decades," Maude said.

"Centuries even," Dorothy said. "She was working for The Other."

"You had a cousin I didn't even know about, and she was working for The Other?" I felt as though my life had been turned upside down. This was all a terrible shock. "But who was that man who was just murdered? Ethelbert? Wasn't he supposed to be her husband?"

Aunt Agnes waved one hand at me. "Oh yes, he would have been one of her husbands. She's had several."

Maude patted my shoulder. "He was killed because he was blackmailing Mrs Mumbles. It had nothing whatsoever to do with The Other."

MORGANA BEST

I rubbed my temples with both hands. "Okay, let me get this straight. Euphemia Jones was your cousin. You haven't seen her in, um, a very long time. She was working for The Other. She used some sort of magic to disguise herself as someone else, someone she called Euphemia Jones."

Aunt Maude butted in. "Yes, that would be the glamour."

I nodded slowly. "Right. So, she came here to spy on you while pretending she was someone wanting to hire one of the cottages." Something occurred to me. "But wait! That doesn't make sense. Her husband came here first, and she only came here *after* he was murdered. She wouldn't have known he was going to be murdered."

"Clearly, she intended to join him here anyway," Aunt Agnes said. "Then she would have found some excuse to stay on. Gorgona always was a nasty piece of work, right from the time she was a child."

Aunt Dorothy nodded vigorously. "She used to bite herself hard on her arm, and she showed our parents the marks. She said we'd bitten her, and we always got into trouble for it."

The other two sisters murmured agreement. They went on with a catalogue of Euphemia-Gorgona's childhood misdeeds while I zoned out, staring at the dead woman on the ground. It was all too much for me. "I need a strong goblet of witches' brew," I said.

Aunt Agnes shook her head. "After the police go."

"And you're saying she was poisoned? Couldn't it have been natural causes?"

Aunt Agnes made a snorting sound. "Of course it wasn't natural causes, Valkyrie. Somebody murdered Gorgona, you mark my words."

"And what motive would The Other have for murdering her?" I asked. "You said she was working for them."

Aunt Maude shrugged one shoulder. "Maybe she asked for more money—who knows? One thing is for certain, she is dead."

CHAPTER 3

*D*etective Oakes and Detective Mason were clearly not impressed that there was another dead body at Mugwort Manor. "You have more murders here than *Rosemary and Thyme*," Detective Mason said, more than a hint of disapproval in his voice.

"*Rosemary and Thyme?*" Aunt Dorothy echoed.

"Yes, they're two women who go around fixing garden problems in a famous TV show," Mason said. "Every time they fix somebody's garden, there is at least one murder. It's just like here. It's a famous TV show," he said again.

"Well, it can't be too famous if I haven't heard of it," Aunt Dorothy said.

"And it's not like here," Aunt Maude protested.

"Sure, Euphemia died in the vegetable patch, but we weren't fixing anybody's garden."

Detective Oakes held up one hand for silence. "The paramedics are on their way. Now, this I take it this is the wife of the victim of the *previous* murder at your establishment?"

Aunt Agnes looked angry, but simply said, "Yes, that's right."

"It was probably natural causes then," Oakes said. "She looks about your age, so she probably died of old age."

Aunt Agnes was struck speechless. Her face turned as red as one of the squashed tomatoes poking out from under Euphemia. I held my breath, but Maude tapped her arm and whispered something in her ear.

Oakes appeared oblivious to the offence his words had caused. He looked up and gasped. "Why is your French niece sitting up a tree?" Breena was still sitting at the top of a tall white gum.

"She's scared of dogs," I said, nodding to Cary. "Even small ones."

"Um, yes, and she's practising for climbing the Eiffel Tower," Aunt Dorothy said.

"She likes abseiling too," Maude hurried to add.

"She enjoys climbing tall trees and abseiling down from them."

Oakes rolled his eyes. "Look, we really didn't need to be called out for this. The woman obviously died from natural causes, given her age."

Detective Mason disagreed with him. "But her husband was murdered, so maybe she was murdered too. He was blackmailing people. Maybe, she was in on it."

Oakes drew him away, and the two spoke. The paramedics arrived moments later and wasted no time bundling the body into the waiting ambulance.

Oakes pulled a notepad out of his pocket. "Now, go over the events of the morning in your own words. What was the first time you saw Euphemia Jones today?"

"When she came over to us just before she died," I said. "She said she had stomach pains, and then she just fell down dead, right into the tomatoes."

"And that was it?" Oakes shot me a suspicious look.

I nodded.

"Did she eat breakfast in your establishment or in her cottage?"

"In her cottage," I said. "We don't serve

breakfast."

Oakes looked puzzled. "But you're a bed and breakfast establishment."

"That's just a figure of speech," Dorothy said. "We supply a variety of milks and also cereals to each guest."

"Then that's breakfast!" Oakes was clearly exasperated.

"But sometimes we provide it in the afternoon," Dorothy protested.

"Did you happen to provide it this morning?" Oakes asked, his expression grim and his pen hovering over his notepad.

I nodded. "Yes, but Euphemia always requested that they be left outside her door. I didn't see her."

"Then show me over to her cottage, if you will."

I took Detective Oakes to the *Game of Thrones* cottage. "This is very unusual," Oakes said, staring at the images on the walls of people's heads being removed. One wall depicted a whole city on fire, and above it, on the ceiling, was a dragon.

"The aunts have themed cottages," I reminded him.

Oakes raised one eyebrow. "And the victim actually *chose* this *Game of Thrones* cottage?"

I shook my head. "No, we usually allocate the

cottages. Her husband was staying in the Retro cottage, and the other cottages weren't ready. We're repainting some of them."

"No doubt they need it," he muttered, looking around. "You stay at the door and don't touch anything." He shot me his best glare before stepping into the cottage.

I did my best to see what I could from where I was standing. The kitchen was partially obscured from view. There was a laptop on the table and various orchids were scattered around. There were also various bottles of herbs. It only occurred to me at that point that the herbs were for witchcraft. I had just thought Euphemia was a keen cook.

"Like I said, it was probably natural causes, but I'm going to ask you not to come back into this cottage until we know for certain," he said.

"Do you know when that would be?" I asked him.

He tapped his chin. "We could probably tell you this afternoon, with any luck."

"Do we notify the next of kin, or do you?" I said.

"Yes, you can notify them, and tell them if they have any questions to give me a call." He pulled a card out of his pocket and handed it to me. "I can see you're unsettled, Ms Jasper. I wouldn't worry. It was probably a heart attack. After all, she didn't appear to be a healthy specimen, and her husband had just passed away. His murder must have been a terrible shock for her. Maybe, her heart just gave out."

"I'm sure you're right," I said, offering him a weak smile.

As soon as the detectives left, Aunt Agnes ushered me inside the manor while muttering rude remarks about Detective Oakes. She promptly left the kitchen. I drank a goblet of witches' brew quickly and then poured myself another. "Do you really think it could have been natural causes?" I asked Maude and Dorothy.

They all shook their heads. "She was a vampire," Aunt Maude said, as if that explained everything.

Aunt Agnes returned and slapped a piece of paper down on the table. "This is her next of kin, along with a contact number."

Aunt Maude snatched up the piece of paper from her and stared at it. "It says 'Ms J. Jones.'"

The aunts exchanged glances. "Jezabeth!" they said in unison.

I raised my eyebrows. "Who is Jezabeth?"

"Gorgona's daughter."

I nodded slowly. "Oh, so your second cousin."

"She is even meaner than Gorgona was," Maude said, clutching Cary to her chest.

"We haven't seen her in many years," Aunt Agnes pointed out. "She could be even more evil by now."

"Do you think she could have killed her mother?" I said.

The aunts shook their heads. "She's not that type of evil," Aunt Agnes said.

I was going to point out that they hadn't seen her in decades, but I thought the better of it. Aunt Agnes was still speaking. "She has issues. I don't know what they are, but I assume she must have them because she is very greedy and narcissistic, highly competitive with everybody, and cold and hard."

Dorothy agreed. "Jezabeth is self-important, and she's also certain she's doing the right thing when she isn't. I'm glad I'm not the one who has to call her."

"Go and do it now, Agnes," Maude said. "It will be like ripping off a Band-Aid. The sooner you do it, the sooner you'll feel better."

Aunt Agnes put her head in her hands. "But

what if Jezabeth comes here?"

"Well, we will have to cross that bridge when we come to it," Maude said. "Agnes, it has to be done." She refilled Aunt Agnes's goblet and pushed it across the table to her. "Here, take this and call her now."

Aunt Agnes sighed but took the goblet and left the room.

"I don't envy her," Dorothy said. "I hope that awful Jezabeth doesn't come here."

"So, is Jezabeth working for The Other too?" I asked them.

"We don't know," Dorothy said. "Gorgona and Jezabeth didn't get on at all. The relationship was quite strained."

"Why was that?" I asked.

Aunt Maude shrugged. "Gorgona's relationship with *everybody* was strained."

"Then Jezabeth won't have any idea who murdered her mother," I pointed out.

There was a scratching sound at the back door, so I walked over to open it. Breena, in cat form, ran inside. Her tail was fluffed up horribly, and she looked startled. I emptied some cat treats into a bowl for her.

"That only encourages her, Valkyrie," Aunt

Maude scolded me. "Breena, can you turn back into human form?"

She meowed and ran out of the room by way of response.

I simply shrugged. "She's very upset," I said, somewhat unnecessarily.

At that point, Aunt Agnes walked back into the room. "That was a difficult conversation. Jezabeth hasn't changed."

"She must have been terribly upset about her mother," I said.

"She hasn't seen her in many years," Aunt Agnes said. "She seemed more interested in coming here to get her mother's possessions. She wanted to know if we knew who Gorgona's lawyer was."

"Lawyer?" I repeated.

"For the will," Agnes said. "I assume she wants to get her hands on her mother's estate as soon as possible."

I was going to ask something, but Aunt Agnes added, "And you won't believe this!"

We waited expectantly. After pausing a moment or two for dramatic effect, she pushed on. "Gorgona has a house in town."

"What? In Lighthouse Bay?" I said. "I thought she lived at Nelson Bay."

Aunt Agnes nodded slowly. "That's what we thought too. Her husband, Ethelbert, lived at Nelson Bay, but Gorgona apparently had a *holiday* house here." Aunt Agnes made air quotes. "From what Jezabeth said, Gorgona lived here all the time."

"She lived in Lighthouse Bay all the time, and you didn't know?" I said in shock. "I mean, I know it has a population of only around forty thousand people, but surely you would have known if your own cousin was in town."

"Our own cousin was staying in one of our *cottages*, and we didn't even know," Aunt Agnes pointed out.

"Did Jezabeth offer any clues as to what happened to her mother?" I asked.

Aunt Agnes shook her head and then said, "No, and we can't mention The Other to Jezabeth. We don't know how much she knows about them, if anything."

Aunt Maude firmly agreed. "Yes, that subject can't come up while Jezabeth is here."

"Where was Jezabeth when you called her?" I asked Aunt Agnes.

"Sydney, and she's taking the first flight to Lighthouse Bay. She'll be here this afternoon."

CHAPTER 4

*W*e all hurried to the *Game of Thrones* cottage to find any evidence of poison. Aunt Agnes had insisted we all wear gloves and had also insisted Dorothy leave Cary inside the manor.

When we reached the cottage, I stood in the doorway and scratched my head. "What exactly are we looking for? I'm sure the murderer didn't leave a bottle with a skull and crossbones on it sitting on a table."

"It might not have been poison," Aunt Dorothy said.

For once, Aunt Agnes agreed with her. "Let's keep an open mind. Still, we have to assume it was poison unless Gorgona was shot with a tiny poisonous dart, but then again, we didn't see any darts sticking out of her. There were no stab or bullet wounds, and she was complaining of violent stomach pains. That, to me, suggests it was poison. Valkyrie, fetch a sample of her witches' brew so we can have it tested for poison."

I crossed to the fridge and looked inside. "There's no wine in here."

"Of course not, Valkyrie. She wasn't going to leave witches' brew out the open, as then we would've known she was a vampire if we happened to look in her fridge. No, it will be disguised as something else."

I pulled out a large bottle labelled as tomato juice, took off the lid, and sniffed it. "Yes, this is witches' brew," I said.

"Okay, we'll take it and test it," Aunt Agnes said. "Let's keep looking through Gorgona's stuff. We don't have much time."

"Actually, if the police rule it natural causes, then we will have plenty of time," Maude pointed out.

Aunt Agnes strongly disagreed. "No, *if* the police do happen to discover it was poison, then they're going to be back here quick smart, and it won't do if we are all in her cottage. They will immediately suspect us."

Aunt Maude rubbed her forehead. "Oh dear. I do believe you're right. All right then, let's hurry."

I ran into the bedroom and opened any drawers I could see, looking for bottles of pills or anything of the like. I found nothing. I heard Aunt Agnes's strident tones from the other room. "Don't touch anything without your gloves. It might've been a poison that killed with contact."

I at once took a step away from the furniture. "Bathroom!" I exclaimed. I hurried into the bathroom but soon emerged rather disappointed. "She doesn't have any moisturiser or cleanser or anything like that. Do you think the poisoner took them?"

"Of course, she didn't have any moisturiser," Aunt Agnes said. "Did you see her face?"

Aunt Dorothy tut-tutted. "Oh Agnes, it's not nice to speak ill of the dead."

Aunt Agnes simply shrugged and continued looking through the contents of the kitchen drawers.

I went back to the bathroom and bagged the Mugwort Manor-supplied hand wash.

Aunt Agnes nodded her approval. "Someone

could easily have put something into that. Remember, sisters and Valkyrie, it might not be something she ingested, so don't discount anything."

I looked under the sofa and then stood up. "We'll have to look into Jezabeth's alibi," I told them. "She says she's coming from Sydney, but maybe she's been in town all the time." I pointed out the window. "Those sand dunes are quite close to this cottage, and there's a lot of cover there. See all those bracken ferns and spinifex? She could easily have slipped in here and poisoned something."

Something else occurred to me. "You know, somebody could have poisoned Gorgona, and then after she left to speak to us, taken the poisoned substance away. We would never have seen them."

"Yes, I thought of that," Aunt Agnes said. "That's entirely possible. Still, I don't think Jezabeth did it."

"But we haven't seen her in a very long time," Aunt Maude said. "And she was a thoroughly nasty person when we last knew her."

"There are plenty of thoroughly nasty people who don't commit murder," Aunt Agnes countered.

Aunt Maude shrugged. "That is true, I'll grant you that, but my point is that if Jezabeth was a thoroughly nasty person a very long time ago, then it's possible her nastiness could have escalated to murder." She waved one finger at Aunt Agnes.

Aunt Agnes did not respond, and we spent the next five minutes searching the remainder of the cottage. As soon as we finished, we took our haul to the aunts' altar room at the top of the stairs and down the long, dark corridor in the manor.

The sound of the doorbell reverberated through the house. "Just in time," Aunt Agnes said. "Quick, all of you out the door."

She ushered us out of the altar room and locked the door behind us. We swept down the stairs and waited while Aunt Agnes opened the front door. A woman, I assume, Jezabeth, was standing on the front steps, her expression impassive.

Jezabeth wasn't what I expected. I wasn't sure exactly what I had expected, but it was certainly not that. She was cold, and while not exactly hostile, she certainly wasn't friendly or pleasant either.

The aunts invited her into the living room and indicated she should sit down. "Would you like tea or coffee?" Aunt Agnes asked her.

"Witches' brew." Her tone was curt.

While Aunt Maude and Aunt Agnes made inconsequential small talk with Jezabeth, I took the opportunity to study her. She was about my height and was quite slender. Her white-blonde hair was worn very short. Her complexion was pale, as were her blue eyes. The expression on her face was pinched. I wondered if it was it always there or whether it was because of her mother's death.

She sipped the potion. "This is quite good witches' brew. You live very close to the Ichor Estate, don't you? Didn't the old guy die overseas?"

Aunt Agnes flushed red. For a minute, I thought she would say Henry Ichor was murdered, but she simply said, "Yes."

"I'm awfully sorry about your mother," I said to change the subject.

She shot me a haughty expression. "We didn't have a good relationship. I see you have a dog. Do you have a cat too?"

The living room doors swung open, and Aunt Dorothy walked in along with Detective Oakes.

I looked up, surprised. "I didn't hear you arrive, Detective Oakes."

He simply nodded to me and looked at Jezabeth. "I'm Detective Oakes," he said.

She simply said, "Okay."

Aunt Agnes hurried to introduce them. "Detective Oakes, this is Jezabeth, Euphemia Jones's daughter."

"I'm sorry for your loss," he said automatically. "I was here to ask the Jasper sisters for the next of kin's contact details, so it's propitious I found you here. I thought I'd let you know that there are no suspicious circumstances. Your mother died of natural causes. This isn't a murder investigation— for once," he added. With that, he offered us all a half smile and turned to leave. Aunt Agnes showed him to the door.

When Aunt Agnes came back to the living room, she said, "You probably all realise by now I have filled in Jezabeth about the matter of her mother's glamour, disguising herself as Euphemia Jones."

"Obviously, she did that to land her last husband, Ethelbert," Jezabeth said in clipped tones. "She had changed her legal name to Euphemia Jones. Still, she was a very strange woman. I couldn't figure out why she did many things. Have you made any progress locating her lawyer?"

"Not yet," Aunt Agnes said.

"I need to stay in one of your cottages. Do you have any vacancies?"

"No," Dorothy said, just as Agnes said, "Yes. Your mother's things are still in the *Game of Thrones* cottage."

"I can't rent that one," Jezabeth said, "not with her dying in there."

Dorothy shook her head. "No, she didn't die in the cottage. She died in our tomato patch, on our best tomatoes."

Jezabeth appeared unmoved. "I see. Well then, what cottage can I have?"

"You could have *The Witcher* cottage," I said. "The decorating isn't finished, but it's the only other possibility." There was also the Jungle Cottage, but it was too nice and too big for the likes of her.

She turned her attention to me. It was all I could do not to shudder. She reminded me of some sort of ghoul. "Did you say The Witches' cottage?"

I shook my head. "No, no. All our cottages are themed. The newest cottage we decorated is *The Witcher* cottage. You know, *The Witcher*, on Netflix?" I sang the chorus of the song.

The aunts and Jezabeth all looked at me as though I had taken leave of my senses. The aunts also plugged their ears. "The song grows on you. Oh well, never mind," I said with a shrug.

"Then I'll grab some paperwork for insurance purposes," Aunt Agnes said. "No charge for the accommodation, of course, because you're our relative."

Jezabeth stood up. "Thanks." She looked at me. "Will you take my suitcase to the cottage?"

"Sure," I said.

"And please have dinner with us tonight," Agnes said.

Jezabeth simply nodded, and I followed her out to her hire car. She didn't say a word to me all the way to the cottage. Clearly, she wasn't one for conversation. I opened the door and handed her the key. She looked at the painting of The Witcher riding his horse across one wall. Her eyes widened, but she didn't comment. "I'll call for you again when I need something," she said.

With that, I was dismissed. I walked as fast as I could without running to the manor and let myself in through the back door. The aunts weren't in the kitchen, so I hurried into the living room where they were all still sitting. "Has Jezabeth settled in?" Aunt Agnes asked me.

"Yes, she seems fine. At least, she's not

complaining. She asked me again if we had any pets other than Cary. If you don't like her, why did you let her have the cottage for free?"

"That's what I just said," Maude said crossly, stroking Cary.

"You know the old saying about keeping your enemies close," Aunt Agnes said. "For all we know, she killed her mother. And on the other hand, if she didn't, we only have her word that she didn't get along with her mother, so maybe they were working together for The Other. We'll have to be quite vigilant, because for all we know, we have an enemy here."

"And possibly a murderer," I said.

Aunt Maude sighed. "Once more, we have to turn our minds to a murder investigation."

"I wouldn't even know where to start this time, to be honest," I said.

Aunt Agnes tapped her chin. "I've been giving this quite a bit of thought. We need to discover whether Gorgona had any enemies."

"She had such an unpleasant personality that she would have had lots of enemies," I pointed out.

"Yes, but surely they all didn't want to kill her," Agnes said.

"They probably did," Dorothy muttered.

"We need to find out about her will. Once we know who her lawyer is, we can find out if there are beneficiaries other than Jezabeth and add them to our list of suspects."

"We don't have a list of suspects," I said. "The only suspect we have is Jezabeth."

Breena walked out from behind the curtains. She was in human form and was clothed for once. She walked over and sat on the high-backed velvet chair. She didn't sit like a person—she sat like a cat would sit.

"Has anyone else noticed that Breena has been acting strangely since Euphemia, I mean Gorgona, was murdered?" Before anyone could respond, I added, "Are you sure it *was* murder? What if she simply did die of natural causes?"

The aunts exchanged glances. "Vampires don't die of natural causes," Aunt Agnes said. "I'm sure we've told you that many a time, Valkyrie."

"No, you haven't," I began, but Aunt Agnes interrupted me.

"She was *murdered*, I can assure you of that. This means we have to investigate her murder to ascertain whether an agent of The Other was involved or whether it was simply a mundane enemy. We will have to make a list of her enemies, and we will have to find out the murder weapon, despite the fact we currently assume it was poison."

"But how are we going to do that?" I said. "What if the substances we took from the cottage test as non-poisonous? The police said Gorgona died from natural causes, so there won't be a toxicology report."

"I've just had a brainwave! Many poisons show up in the hair," Aunt Agnes said, clearly pleased with herself. "We'll have to go to the funeral and take some of Gorgona's hair."

"What if it isn't an open casket?" I said.

Aunt Agnes tapped her head. "Yes, well, that will make things somewhat more difficult. Stop that, Breena!"

I looked over at Breena, who was sitting on her haunches, scratching the velvet fabric of the chair on which she had just been sitting.

"You have a scratching post in your bedroom," Aunt Agnes said. To me, she said, "It's quite simple, really. First, we make a list of suspects. Next, we send off the substances we took from the cottage to a lab, and if they all test negative, we take some of Gorgona's hair to have it analysed for poisons."

I was lost for words. Had Aunt Agnes completely lost her mind? That seemed more difficult than the labours of Hercules. Just what was I going to do?

"Oh, and I almost forgot," Aunt Agnes continued. "If an agent of The Other did murder Gorgona, then one of us might be next on the list."

CHAPTER 5

"I've just had a call from a lawyer!" Aunt Agnes announced. "Bentley Harper."

I looked up from my third cup of coffee. "What? He called you so early?"

"It's nine in the morning, Valkyrie."

I rubbed my temples. I had awoken with a groggy headache and was hitting the coffee hard in an attempt to shift it. "What did he say?" I spread some Vegemite on a piece of toast and sat at the kitchen table.

"Well, you won't believe this!"

We all looked at her expectantly. She smiled at each one of us in turn before continuing. "He was Gorgona's lawyer—of course, he thought her name was Euphemia Jones. It turns out that we are the executors of the will!" Her voice rose to a high pitch.

"Who is?" Maude asked.

"You, me, and Dorothy," Aunt Agnes said. "He didn't mention Jezabeth."

"Does that mean she wasn't left anything in her mother's will?" Aunt Maude leant across the table.

"We'll know soon enough," she said. "He's on his way here. He wants to talk to us and Jezabeth as well."

"Did he ask to speak to anyone else?" Maude asked.

Aunt Agnes shook her head. "No, so it looks as though there are no other beneficiaries."

Maude adjusted Cary on her lap. "Why is he coming here instead of us going to his office?"

Aunt Agnes pointed to me. "So Valkyrie can overhear, of course. She can hide in the secret room and listen in. I told the lawyer that Dorothy was old and infirm and wouldn't be able to make it to his office."

Dorothy's cheeks turned as red as a tomato. "Well, you have got some nerve!"

"Enough of your protesting," Aunt Agnes said. "You'll have to act old and infirm, or he will suspect something is amiss. Now, we don't have much time.

One of us will have to fetch Jezabeth, while Valkyrie hides in the secret room."

"Do I have enough time to put on some make-up and some nice clothes, do you think?" Dorothy asked her.

"Just stay as you are, Dorothy," Aunt Agnes snapped. "I don't think he wants to date you."

"Well then, I'll go and fetch Jezabeth!"

Aunt Agnes stepped in front of her to forestall her. "You can't! You're old and infirm, remember? Go into the living room now and sit on a chair and try to look ill or something, or maybe upset."

"Then I won't have to act," Dorothy snapped. She stomped out of the room.

"I'll go and fetch Jezabeth," Maude said.

Agnes nodded. "And I'll take Valkyrie to the secret room." She escorted me to the room, in which I had been several times of late as it led to the passageway between Mugwort Manor and Henry Ichor's estate, which was now owned by Lucas. Henry was Lucas's deceased uncle. Apparently, Aunt Agnes and Henry had a dalliance some years ago, hence the tunnel, or so Aunt Agnes said. My parents had been hiding out at Henry's estate and I'd been meeting them in the tunnel.

"Observe Jezabeth carefully," Aunt Agnes said

to me. "She could be an innocent person, but she could be the murderer or she could be working for The Other. Maybe she is the murderer *and* working for The Other."

"What exactly am I looking for?"

Aunt Agnes shrugged. "Just keep an eye on her and see if anything occurs to you. Now, where's that cat? I should put her in the secret room with you."

"Please don't," I said.

Before Agnes could answer, a cat landed on the floor next to me. "Thanks for nothing!" I called after Aunt Agnes' departing back.

The cat once morphed into a woman, a naked woman.

A bathrobe flew into the secret room and then I heard the door lock. "Thanks. I mean it sincerely this time," I called after Aunt Agnes, but I knew she wouldn't hear me. The secret room was soundproofed, although sound fed inside it via a sound system from the living room.

"Hi, Breena," I said.

She looked startled that I spoke to her. Although she was spending more time in human form, she had not abandoned all of her cat ways. She sat on the ground and licked her hand and then rubbed it over her head. I shrugged and looked through the two-way mirror.

Aunt Dorothy was sitting in the room, looking quite put out. I was already bored and wished I'd brought in some snacks. I tried the door, but sadly Aunt Agnes had locked me in.

I wasn't bored for long. Jezabeth and Aunt Maude walked into the room. Aunt Maude manoeuvred it so Jezabeth sat facing me. I thought it a clever move, because I would be able to see her expression. There was still no sign of the lawyer. As I was silently lamenting that fact, Aunt Agnes walked in with a man. I couldn't guess his age, but he had thick black hair. He shook Jezabeth's hand and then Maude's hand and I smiled when Dorothy limply offered him her hand.

I turned up the volume so I could hear what they were saying clearly.

"I have the original will here," the man said. "I suggest you make several copies. Have any of you been executors before?"

I saw them all shake their heads, although I wondered if that were true.

"When you apply for probate, you will need to submit the original will. However, you might need certified copies of the will for various services like phone, electricity, Internet, and so on. Those places usually only need a certified copy of the death certificate, but you won't have to give the original death certificate to anyone."

"Where do I get a copy of the death certificate from?" Jezabeth asked him.

"It will be sent to you in the mail. You will arrange that with the funeral director," he said. "Have you selected a funeral director yet?"

Jezabeth looked quite put out. "No," was all she said.

"Then a funeral director will arrange the death certificate for you," he said. "It can take two to three weeks to be posted to your house."

He stood up and handed some papers to Agnes. "This is the original will."

"Shouldn't I have that?" asked Jezabeth.

The lawyer sat back down. "I'm afraid not. There are only three executors of the will, Agnes Jasper, Maude Jasper, and Dorothy Jasper. I'm afraid you're not an executor."

I wondered if Jezabeth would explode. Her face grew whiter and whiter. She gripped both arms of the antique grandfather chair in which she was sitting. "Why not?" she demanded in an icy tone.

"The will doesn't specify," he said. "Now, as for

the contents of the will, you are a beneficiary. The beneficiaries are the Jasper sisters, you, your daughter, and Euphemia's great niece, Belladonna Shadowsoul."

Jezabeth stood up. "Belladonna," she spat. "I haven't seen her in years. Do you have an address for her?"

The lawyer shook his head. "No, I'm afraid I don't."

"Then can she get anything if you don't have an address for her?" Jezabeth snapped.

"Yes, it's still legally hers. The fact you don't know where she is has no relevance," the lawyer said patiently. He gestured to the papers. "As you can see for yourselves, the terms of the will state that you and the Jasper sisters have an equal share of all the antiques and of Euphemia's jewellery and house contents, but her house at Lighthouse Bay is to be sold. You and Belladonna are each to receive twenty percent of the sale proceeds of the house. The remaining sixty percent is to be deposited in an offshore account."

Once more, Jezabeth jumped to her feet. "An offshore account! What kind of hocus-pocus is this?"

The lawyer held up one hand, palm outwards.

"I'm just the messenger, so to speak. Your mother didn't discuss any terms with me."

"What about the money in her bank?" Jezabeth asked.

"Your daughter, Hemlock, receives one hundred and twenty thousand pounds. The remainder of the money in your mother's bank account is to be deposited into the same offshore account," the lawyer said. "Of course, you can withdraw money from that for the funeral. That's permissible under the terms. The executors can simply make an application to the bank to cover the funeral expenses and the burial plot."

"But what about her house at Nelson Bay?" Jezabeth asked. "Who gets that?"

The lawyer looked surprised. "I'm sorry, I didn't realise you didn't know. Your mother has already sold it."

"Who gets that money?" Even from where I was looking through a two-way mirror, I could see Jezabeth had turned as white as a ghost. Her eyes were bloodshot and veins had popped up on her face.

"I assume that the monies were deposited into your mother's bank account. At any rate, your mother gave instructions for me to transfer the balance of her bank account into an offshore account upon her death," he said.

"Could I offer you a cup of tea or coffee?" Aunt Agnes asked him. "It was awfully good of you to come out here in consideration for my sister's health."

Right on cue, Dorothy bent over and went into a series of hacking coughs. It seemed a case of overacting to me and Aunt Agnes must've thought so too, because she walked over and slapped her hard on the back.

"A cup of coffee would be nice, please," the lawyer said when Dorothy stopped coughing.

"I'll have wine," Jezabeth said. If the lawyer thought it strange that she would drink wine that early in the morning, he didn't show it. And, of course, he didn't realise it was witches' brew, not ordinary wine.

Agnes nodded. "Maude will help me. Come on, Maude."

The two of them left the room and Dorothy pretended to fall asleep. She leant back, her eyes shut, and snored gently. It was all I could do not to burst into a fit of giggles at her fake snores, although they did sound pretty good.

I figured the aunts had left to see if there would be any interaction between Jezabeth and the lawyer.

"Are you sure that's the latest will?" Jezabeth asked him as soon as Agnes and Maude had left the room.

"Yes, certainly," he said.

"And what about my daughter, Hemlock? Surely, my mother left her something else in the will? Poor Hemlock is too sensitive to get a job, so she needs money, a *lot* of money. She has expensive tastes, you see. I'm afraid I've had to cut her off, so she needs to get money from somewhere."

He shook his head. "I'm sorry, there are no terms other than what I have mentioned."

Jezabeth simply glared at him. Breena was now standing up, looking through the two-way mirror with me. Just as I was thinking she was beginning to act like a person, she hissed at Jezabeth.

"I don't much like her either," I said to Breena. "She seems as bad as her mother."

The lawyer and Jezabeth didn't speak again until the aunts came back into the room.

After the lawyer finished his coffee, he gave the aunts some papers to sign. From what I understood, they were statements to verify they had received the original will.

Jezabeth tried one more time. "You're sure it was the latest will?" Before the lawyer could respond, she added, "And are you sure nothing else was left for my daughter, Hemlock?"

When the lawyer shook his head, she added, "That's just not right. My mother loved my daughter. She promised her that she would leave her a substantial amount in the will. In fact, every time my daughter asked her what she was being left in the will, my mother told her that she would do *very* well out of it."

"Hemlock sounds just as bad as her mother and grandmother," I said to Breena.

Breena hissed in response.

CHAPTER 6

"Seriously, her daughter's name is Hemlock?" I asked Aunt Agnes. "Who on earth would call a child Hemlock? It's a poisonous plant."

"So is Belladonna," Aunt Agnes said, "and I hear Hemlock herself is very fond of plants." She made a smoking motion.

It took me a while to catch on. "Oh, I see. She's a stoner."

Aunt Dorothy looked up. "A stoner? What's that?"

"Keep up with the modern times, Dorothy," Aunt Agatha scolded her. "A stoner is someone who smokes a lot of weed."

Aunt Dorothy's brow furrowed in confusion.

"Who would smoke weeds? Oh! I see." She nodded slowly.

"Is this Hemlock woman going to turn up anytime soon?" I asked, throwing up my hands to the ceiling.

"I hope not," Aunt Agnes said, "but I doubt it. Last I heard, she lives in Adelaide. Now, we must prepare for our dinner tonight with Jezabeth. We can't trust her, you know, as she's a vampire and also a witch, just like her mother."

"Am I the only one here who finds it suspicious that she didn't come to dinner last night when she was invited?" I asked. "And will Linda be safe having dinner with her?"

Aunt Agnes shook her head. "I really don't like Linda having dinner with a vampire such as Jezabeth, who could well be working for The Other. After all, The Other wants to wipe out all shifters."

Breena let out a plaintiff meow.

Aunt Agnes shook her finger at her. "You can't let her know you're a shifter, Breena. It would be awfully dangerous. You either stay in your human form and we'll have to make up some excuse about you, or you remain as a cat. Really, you will have to make your choice now and stay that way while Jezabeth is here."

Breena was currently in human form, so she simply nodded. To my surprise, she said, "Human. Not cat."

Agnes shot her a look of approval. "Okay then, we will have to come up with your cover story. What could it be?"

"We told the police she was our niece from France," Dorothy said.

Aunt Agnes paused from stacking the dishwasher. "That won't do at all. Jezabeth will know at once that she's not our niece from France. We will have to say she's one of the boarders." She clapped her hands. "That's it! We'll say she is one of the boarders and that she's French and doesn't speak much English."

"But what if Jezabeth speaks French?" I asked. "And if we tell her that Breena's one of the boarders, how will we explain why she's staying in the house and not in a cottage?'

Aunt Agnes slammed the dishwasher door shut and clutched her head with both hands. "Of course! Oh dear, what will we do?"

Maude cleared her throat. "Look, Jezabeth doesn't seem one for conversation, and she couldn't care less about anyone but herself. Why don't we tell Breena to respond with short, one-word answers and not to get drawn into any conversation? The rest of us can help deflect."

"I'm sure that could work," Aunt Agnes said, although her tone suggested otherwise.

"And Linda can help us," I said. "I explained everything to her when I called to tell her Euphemia Jones had died."

Aunt Agnes almost dropped the jar of Vegemite. "What? It wasn't all over town already?"

"If it was, it hadn't reached Linda," I said.

"But what excuse will we give for Linda's presence tonight?" Maude asked.

"The truth, of course," I said. "We'll say she's a friend of mine, because she is."

"I need a strong glass of witches' brew," Aunt Agnes said, holding her the back of her hand across her forehead in a melodramatic fashion. "I'm sure this dinner is going to be the most complete disaster."

"It won't be as bad as tomorrow," Maude pointed out. "Tomorrow we have to go to Euphemia's house and see what kind of state it's in, and sort through all her stuff and then get it ready for sale."

"Maybe you could have Linda as the selling agent."

Aunt Agnes turned to me. "Does she have her real estate licence yet?"

I nodded and then shook my head. "She has the type of licence she needs to work for somebody else," I told her. "She's just started working for one of the real estate firms in town."

Thankfully, I didn't see Jezabeth for the rest of the day. I did see her hire car leave the manor. She was away for several hours and I wondered what she could possibly be doing. I spent the day in the office catching up on long-overdue paperwork. I had intended to do some more painting in *The Witcher* cottage, but the day was cold and drizzly, and I didn't think the paint would dry too well.

Later that afternoon, I helped the aunts prepare dinner. It was to be held in the formal dining room. "We'll need to increase the protection around the room, what with that evil wench here," Aunt Maude said.

"What are those you holding?" I asked.

The three aunts gasped in unison.

"You don't know what these are?" Aunt Maude said, holding them out for me to inspect. "Honestly, Valkyrie, your education is sadly lacking. I thought we would have shown you what these are. They're rusty railroad spikes."

I stared at them. "Oh yes, so they are. I thought you had some at the boundaries of the property?"

The aunts nodded solemnly. "Yes, we do," Aunt Maude said, "but we're going to put them around the dining room too. We can't be too careful, not with Jezabeth here."

"What other protective measures are we going to take?" I asked her.

"Well, after she leaves, we're going to wipe everything she touched, the table, and the chair in which she sits, with Florida Water to cleanse it," Aunt Dorothy said, "and we will mop the floors with lemongrass."

"Valkyrie asked about *preventative* measures," Aunt Agnes said.

Dorothy appeared unperturbed. "Sure. We'll be burning Fiery Wall of Protection incense," she said, pointing to a charcoal disc in a cauldron in the corner of the room. I knew Fiery Wall of Protection incense consisted of frankincense and myrrh, as well as the Indonesian red tree resin known as Dragon's Blood.

Aunt Agnes nodded. "And we'll do the usual, like having eucalyptus leaves in our shoes and wearing evil eye bracelets on our left wrists." She tapped herself on the head. "Oh, I almost forgot.

We have to bring in more of our tourmaline, black agate, and labradorite crystals and place them around the room. The more, the merrier. Valkyrie, can you help me in here with our big painting of Saint Michael?"

I followed her out of the room and into the magnificent entry hall. Hanging on the wood panelling next to an imposing bronze statue of a woman in Grecian drapes was a large painting of Saint Michael in a huge gilded frame. A ladder was already standing under it. Aunt Agnes shimmied up the ladder. "Help me, would you, Valkyrie? It's heavy."

Somehow, the two of us managed to lower the painting to the parquetry floor unscathed. The frame indeed was very heavy. We struggled with the painting to the living room. "Can't we leave it on the floor?" I said hopefully.

Aunt Agnes shook her head vigorously. "No, it needs to hang directly opposite Jezabeth. Saint Michael is very protective. He's been used in many traditions, including Hoodoo, for protection. Valkyrie, would you be a dear and bring that ladder in here for me?"

I sighed and walked back to the foyer. I picked up the stepladder and brought it back to the dining room where I set it up again. "You go up the ladder this time, Valkyrie," said Aunt Agnes. "I will lift the painting up to you."

More than ever, I wished Lucas were here. The big, bulky painting was difficult to manoeuvre onto the hooks, but finally I managed. The aunts stood back and directed me to adjust it several times until it was straight.

Aunt Agnes handed me a Saint Michael medallion. "Keep this in your pocket at all times," she said.

"If Jezabeth poisoned her mother, do you think she'll try to poison us?" I asked them.

I expected the aunts to make fun of my suggestion, but they all nodded solemnly. "It *is* quite possible," Aunt Agnes said in agreement. "Don't take your eyes off your food at any time in case she slips something into it, and if she brings any wine, we'll pour it into her glass first and make sure she finishes it."

I was beginning to think it wasn't safe for Linda to come, after all, but with her new job as a real estate agent keeping her busy, I hadn't had a chance to catch up with her lately. Besides, she was a shifter wolf and so she was cunning. I felt certain she would be safe.

"Well, we can't have any tomatoes tonight, what with Euphemia squashing them all," Dorothy said as she inspected the vegetable garden.

I had walked over to my cottage to dress for dinner and then returned. I wanted to be there early. And it was just as well I was, because the front door bell rang as soon as Dorothy and I walked back inside the manor.

Aunt Agnes looked at the time on her phone. "If that's Jezabeth, she's early. Well, no matter, we can have drinks in the living room. Remember, don't leave your food or drink unattended around her in case she poisons it. I'm sure she'd have no motive to do so, but we can't be too careful."

We all followed Agnes to the front door. Indeed, Jezabeth was standing on the porch. She thrust a box of chocolates at Agnes. "Thanks for inviting me," she said in clipped tones.

"Please come into the living room," Aunt Agnes said. "We're having witches' brew with dinner, so would you like some now or maybe champagne?"

"Champagne," Jezabeth said.

The aunts showed her inside. "It's good that you're early," Aunt Agnes began, "because we wanted to have a little chat with you before the other dinner guests arrived."

Jezabeth looked surprised. "Other guests?" she repeated.

"Yes, Breena, one of our current boarders, and Linda, an old friend of Valkyrie's."

Jezabeth wrinkled her nose in obvious disgust. Aunt Agnes pushed on. "We were concerned that the police have ruled your mother's cause of death as natural. We are concerned that she was, in fact, murdered."

Jezabeth's hand flew to her throat. "Murdered?" she repeated. After a moment, she added, "What utter nonsense! She wasn't murdered!" It was the first time I had heard her raise her voice. She looked furious.

"The other guests don't know about us," Aunt Agnes said, gesturing to each one of us and Jezabeth in turn. "I couldn't discuss it in front of them, but vampires don't die of natural causes."

"What nonsense!" Jezabeth said again. "She had a heart condition."

"Vampires can have heart conditions?" I asked.

Jezabeth shot me a look of pure malice. "My mother did."

Aunt Agnes tried again. "We are all concerned as we suspect that your mother was poisoned.

Wouldn't you like to have a toxicology report on your mother just to prove she wasn't murdered?"

"Absolutely not!" Jezabeth spat. "This is just making it also much harder. My poor mother." She pulled a tissue out of her bag and dabbed at her eyes. She wasn't at all a good actor, and I wondered if she had ever felt any emotion apart from anger. "I won't have it!" she hissed. "Probate can't begin if there's a murder investigation."

Aha. So that was the reason—even if she thought perhaps her mother had been murdered, she didn't want her share of the inheritance to be delayed by a murder investigation. But was that the sole reason? What if she was, in fact, the murderer?

The doorbell rang. Aunt Agnes left the room and returned with Linda and Breena arm in arm. We had arranged for Linda to keep close to Breena. This time, Breena looked more like a human and less like a cat. Aunt Agnes had given her a long talk that afternoon about not meowing or hissing or sitting on someone's lap or lapping her food from the table. I certainly hoped it would work. Still, Breena had seemed more like a human and less like a cat in the last day.

Aunt Agnes introduced them. Jezabeth simply nodded at Linda and Breena and did not look the slightest bit interested, much to my relief. After Aunt Dorothy and Aunt Maude left the room, the conversation was minimal, non-existent even. Thankfully, the aunts returned presently and announced dinner was ready.

"Would you like some more champagne?" Agnes asked Jezabeth.

"No. I'll have wine."

Agnes poured everyone except Linda and Breena some witches' brew. "Linda, would you like your usual champagne?"

She poured Linda a glass of champagne and poured a glass of milk for Breena.

Jezabeth made a snorting sound. "Is she drinking milk?" She addressed the question to Agnes.

"She's a health fanatic," Agnes said.

Jezabeth seemed to accept the lie and at once seemed to lose interest in Breena. She nodded to Cary. "Does that dog get on well with the cats?"

"We don't have any cats," I said, wondering why she said that.

"I'm sorry about your mother's death," Linda said to Jezabeth.

"Did you know her?" Jezabeth asked.

"I'd met her a few times," Linda said. "I used to

be a boarder here. That's how I became friends with Pepper."

Jezabeth frowned. "Pepper? Who is Pepper?"

I pointed to myself. "I'm Pepper. The aunts insist on calling me Valkyrie, however."

Jezabeth looked quite put out. "Then what's your name?"

"Pepper," Linda and I said in unison.

"Valkyrie," said the aunts.

Jezabeth muttered something to herself. I didn't hear the words, but I imagined they weren't complimentary.

Thankfully, Jezabeth wasn't one for conversation. She didn't initiate any conversation throughout the first course. I also noted she didn't eat much, although she did drink a lot of witches' brew.

"Is there any food left over?" she suddenly asked at the end of the first course.

"Do you want more?" I said. "You haven't eaten half of what's on your plate."

She looked quite affronted. "It's not for me, it's for Hemlock."

"Hemlock?" Linda shrieked. "The deadly plant?"

I kicked Linda under the table. "Hemlock is Jezabeth's daughter."

"Oh." Linda looked shocked. "What a pretty name," she said lamely.

"But isn't Hemlock in Adelaide?" Aunt Agnes said.

"No, she should be here any minute," Jezabeth pronounced.

A collective gasp went up around the table. "Here any minute?" Aunt Agnes echoed. "Whatever do you mean?"

"When I told Hemlock about her being a beneficiary in the will, I suggested she move here and live in my mother's house while we get it ready for sale. It will be a tremendous help to us all."

The aunts were visibly shocked. "But we're the executors," Aunt Agnes pointed out in even tones. "That is, I'm an executor, Dorothy is an executor, and Maude is an executor. You're not an executor, so you can't make decisions about what happens to the house."

"But it will be a wonderful benefit to us," Jezabeth said in a monotone. "The house won't be robbed with someone in it, and Hemlock can clean the place for us. It will be a wonderful benefit for all of us," she said again.

I could see the aunts were furious and were doing their best not to show it. "But it's not legal," Aunt Agnes said. "We're the executors and we haven't given our approval. Why, you haven't even asked us!"

Jezabeth waved one hand at them. "I knew you wouldn't mind, so I didn't bother to ask you. It will help everybody to have Hemlock living there." The doorbell rang. "That must be Hemlock now. Well Agnes, are you going to answer the door?"

If looks could kill! Aunt Agnes's expression was entirely murderous. She stormed out of the dining room. Linda and I exchanged glances. I could see Linda was doing her best not to laugh, but I was furious. The nerve of Jezabeth! I couldn't believe anybody could have such a sense of entitlement.

Aunt Agnes returned with a young woman I could only assume was Hemlock. She was short and had clearly applied her make up with a trowel, and no doubt in a dark room at that. I had never seen such thick eyeliner on anyone, and there were large black smudges under her eyes. The pungent odor of illegal substances hung around her like a cloud. "Mother!" she exclaimed, hurrying over to give Jezabeth a hug.

Jezabeth did not return the hug, but stood there,

79

her hands by her sides. "You can stay with me here in the cottage tonight, and in the morning, I'll drive you into town and settle you into your house," she said to Hemlock.

I looked at Aunt Agnes to see if she would explode. She was already letting Jezabeth stay here for free and now she had two boarders. Once more, Jezabeth hadn't even asked.

"Sit down and have some dinner, Hemlock," Jezabeth said. "You're just in time for dessert, but you'd better eat some of your first course before that. How was your flight?"

"It was a good thing the taxi knew where to find this place out the middle of nowhere," Hemlock said, her speech slurred. "What do youse do for fun around here?"

Jezabeth did not respond but introduced us. "You know the aunts, of course, and this is their niece, who calls herself Valkyrie or Pepper— strange, I know—and this is her friend, Linda, and this is a guest." She addressed Breena. "I forgot your name."

Breena simply looked at her. I said, "Breena."

"Hi!" Hemlock said. "When can I see my new house?"

"It isn't *your* house, Hemlock," Aunt Agnes said

firmly. "It's going up for sale, so you will need to keep it absolutely spotless. Also, you'll need to be absent when the real estate agent shows the house. Those are the only conditions under which we will allow you in the house. Do you understand?"

"Yeah, whatever. I'll do whatever youse like." Hemlock reached for a goblet of witches' brew and drank it in one gulp. She burped. "Do youse have any more?"

CHAPTER 7

"Karen Cosgrove!" Aunt Agnes exclaimed as soon as the guests had left.

"Who? What?" I said, confused.

"She's Killian Cosgrove's wife," Aunt Agnes said. "As we know, Gorgona's husband, Ethelbert, was blackmailing Mrs Mumbles and her lover, Killian Cosgrove. Maybe she was blackmailing Killian's wife, Karen, too. Maybe Karen was even involved in Ethelbert's murder, for all we know."

"Why didn't I think of that?" I said.

Aunt Maude walked over. "One of the detectives did mention it."

"Then we have someone to add to our suspects list," I said. "Now we have Jezabeth and Karen."

"How are we going to investigate Karen?" asked Aunt Agnes. "I suppose we could go for another pedicure."

"Count me out this time," I said firmly. "Anyway, why did you allow Hemlock to live in Gorgona's house?"

"We didn't have a choice, really," Aunt Agnes said. "Jezabeth is a thoroughly nasty person. If we hadn't allowed her daughter free range on the house, then she might have burnt it down or something."

"Surely not!" I was in a state of disbelief.

The aunts shrugged. "Anything is possible with Jezabeth," Aunt Dorothy said. "She's incredibly narcissistic and has a huge level of entitlement. Besides, *nothing* is ever her fault. It doesn't matter what she does, she always blames somebody else."

"But won't Hemlock make a terrible mess of the house?" I asked them.

"It doesn't really matter to us because we don't get any proceeds of the house," Maude said.

Aunt Agnes disagreed. "Well, there's Belladonna. We have to make sure she gets her fair share. And although we can't do anything about it, I'm quite concerned about the money that is going into the offshore account. No doubt it's to fund The Other."

It was beginning to dawn on me. "So that's why you're letting Hemlock move into the house. It could be a good thing—it will sell for less because it will be a terrible mess, and so there will be less money for The Other."

Aunt Agnes nodded slowly. "I do admit that it crossed my mind, but I still have to do the right thing by Belladonna."

"Where *is* Belladonna?" I asked.

Aunt Agnes shrugged. "As far as I know, nobody has seen her in years, decades even. She's Gorgona's great niece."

"Then what happens if she never comes forward to claim her inheritance?"

"That's a matter for the lawyers," Aunt Agnes said. "I'm sure Bentley Harper will see to it. And even if he doesn't, it's his problem, not ours," she said with a dismissive wave of her hand.

I went to bed that night, somewhat irritated. I couldn't believe the nerve of Jezabeth, and her daughter, Hemlock, was just as bad.

When I awoke the next morning, the sun was streaming through the windows. I jumped out of bed and rubbed my eyes before looking at my phone. I had slept in. I showered and dressed and hurried to the manor, desperate for coffee.

When I let myself in through the back door, the aunts were sitting at the kitchen table. "We've been deciding what to do about Jezabeth and Hemlock and the house," Aunt Agnes said.

"Did you come up with anything?" I asked.

"No, not any solutions," Aunt Agnes said. "As soon as you've had breakfast, we'll head over to the house and assess the situation."

"Will I call Linda to meet us there?" I asked.

Aunt Agnes shook her head. "No, not quite yet. We need to do some snooping first and see if there are any incriminating papers. Don't forget, Gorgona didn't expect to be murdered, so she could have left something incriminating around her house."

"Her house was likely magically protected as well," Aunt Maude pointed out. "We'll need to take protection with us."

I drank three cups of coffee in quick succession and ate some Vegemite toast. "Okay, I'm ready," I said. "Breena, are you coming with us?"

She looked terrified and shook her head.

Agnes tapped her arm. "Okay, you can stay here, but you mustn't leave the manor. Is that understood?"

Breena nodded.

"It's not safe if Jezabeth and Hemlock see you without us around," Aunt Agnes continued, "so even if they knock or bang on the door, you're not to answer it or go outside. Maybe draw the curtains in the living room and stay in there and watch Netflix until we get back."

Breena readily agreed.

"Wait, are you eating toast?" I asked her.

She nodded and gingerly chewed on the end of a piece of toast.

"She's becoming more of a person and less of a cat every day," I said in surprise.

I was also surprised when we reached Gorgona's house. I had expected it to be somewhere in the middle of town or even on the edge of town, an unremarkable house on an unremarkable suburban street. I was shocked to see the sprawling mansion high up on a hill with a wonderful view of one of the Lighthouse Bay beaches.

"What! Why, why, it's a mansion!" I stammered.

I looked at Aunt Dorothy, who was sitting next

MORGANA BEST

to me in the back seat. Her jaw was hanging open too.

"I wonder what her husband thought of her living in a mansion like this while he lived in an ordinary house in Nelson Bay," I said.

Aunt Agnes chuckled. "I don't think she would have given him a chance to voice his opinion. He was a human, not a vampire, so he would have done whatever she said."

Something occurred to me. "Is Hemlock a vampire?"

"She's a lot of things," Aunt Agnes said in disgust, "and, yes, a vampire is one of them."

"I wouldn't get on her wrong side, if I were you," Aunt Dorothy continued. "She's not the sharpest tool in the shed if you get my meaning, and she's also highly opinionated. Put those together and you have someone who is a bit of a problem."

Aunt Agnes snorted. "A *bit* of a problem! Why, I remember when she was a child, she would have the most dreadful tantrums. She would even scream at her mother."

Aunt Maude readily agreed. "And she often stole money from her mother."

"Yes, that's why I watched her all the time over dinner," Aunt Maude said. "I didn't want the family silver disappearing into her handbag."

"Oh well, let's get out and have a good snoop around the house," Aunt Agnes said. "And I'm going to lock the door behind me so when Jezabeth and Hemlock arrive, they won't be able to get in and catch us snooping."

"It isn't really snooping, is it?" I pointed out. "The three of you are executors. You're legally entitled to look around."

Agnes grunted. "Common sense and Jezabeth don't have anything in common."

We got out of the truck we had hired in the expectation of having boxes of paperwork to remove. I paused halfway up the steps to look down at the beach far below us. "What an absolutely beautiful view," I said, gesturing to the expanse of white sand and the sparkling sea below us. "Oh look, there's a boat out on the horizon. Gorgona would've had a wonderful view of dolphins and whales from here."

I looked around to see the aunts were already at the top of the stairs, standing outside the front door. Aunt Agnes was beckoning to me. I hurried up to the door. It was painted a muted shade of red and covered with Chinese emblems in gold. "Those are spells," Aunt Agnes said. She rubbed a potion on them before turning the key in the lock.

As she opened the door, I gasped. I had imagined Euphemia would have an old-fashioned house. I had always also thought she would be messy and a hoarder, like one of those people you see on TV. Nothing could have been further from the truth.

The white marble floors, high ceilings, huge windows, and white walls all screamed sleek, modern design. Huge potted plants supplied a pop of colour. However, incongruous with the modernity of the architecture were the numerous antiques: five boules, one huge lavabo, numerous cedar chiffonieres, and all manner of upholstered Victorian chairs and chaises as well as earlier chairs that looked to my untrained eye to be Hepplewhite. Marble-topped credenzas were covered by Victorian glassware of every shape and colour, and garish works of majolica sat on all the coffee tables.

"Wow, this house is so big!" I exclaimed. "Where on earth would someone hide something in here? It's so big, I wouldn't even know where to look."

"Let's start in the study, once we find it," Aunt Agnes said. "Let's all spread out and then whoever finds the study, call out. First of all, we have to bring in all the boxes from the truck."

Aunt Maude was the one who found the study. It was upstairs and sported huge picture windows affording magnificent views of the ocean. "Okay, Valkyrie and I will look through stuff in here," Aunt Agnes said. "You two go to the garage and see if you can find a safe. If you find one, use magic to open it."

"But it would be magically protected," Aunt Dorothy protested.

"Duh!" Aunt Agnes said. "So then, use magic to break that magical protection." She rolled her eyes and turned back to the study, muttering rudely to herself.

Aunt Agnes turned to me. "Go through all the paperwork, and tell me if you find anything even remotely suspicious. Leave electricity bills, phone bills, and Internet bills and the like here, but take anything else, unless they are receipts for printers and stuff like that. We have to take everything else. And don't waste too much time. If in doubt, throw it in the boxes."

I did as she asked. I rifled through paper after

paper. I found a bunch of old photos, which I threw in the box at my feet.

Aunt Agnes and I were packing the second box when Aunt Maude and Aunt Dorothy burst into the room. "You'll never guess what we found in the safe!" Maude said, her eyes wide in horror.

CHAPTER 8

"What did you find?" I asked.

Aunt Maude shoved a bunch of photographs at me as well as a DVD case. "I'm afraid the case is empty, but there's an image on the cover."

Aunt Agnes put a hand over my eyes. "Valkyrie's not even a hundred years old yet! You can't show that to her!"

"Why not?" I protested, managing to push her hand away. I stared at the cover of the DVD tape in shock. "Is that Karen Killian? And who's that man she's with?"

"It's obviously a sex tape," Aunt Agnes said. "It was just as I thought! Gorgona and Ethelbert were blackmailing Karen as well."

"And we can add that man to our suspects list," I said.

Aunt Agnes peered at the photo. "We'll need a magnifying glass."

"That's rather unkind, Agnes!" Aunt Maude said.

Aunt Agnes rolled her eyes. "For his face, Maude."

Aunt Maude looked embarrassed. "Oh yes, I see."

"Well, I'm pleased that we have another suspect, at any rate," I said.

"Was there anything else in the safe?" Agnes asked the other aunts. "Jewellery? Valuables?"

They shook their heads. "Just all these photographs and that DVD," Aunt Maude said. "There are lots of photos of Killian Cosgrove and Mrs Mumbles as well."

"We know about those," Agnes said. "What a shame the DVD case is empty."

"We found lots of loose DVDs and put them in a box. Maybe one of those is the sex tape." Aunt Dorothy handed a piece of paper to Agnes. "Oh, and we weren't sure what this meant."

I looked over Aunt Agnes's shoulder. "What does it say?"

Aunt Agnes handed the paper to me. "It says Joyce Batson was late with a payment."

I raised my eyebrows. "A payment? Does that mean they were blackmailing her too?"

Agnes shrugged. "It seems like it, unless maybe they sold her an expensive antique and she was paying it off. I'll have to question Joyce."

I knew Aunt Agnes was fond of the local antique dealer, so I fervently hoped she wasn't the murderer. It seemed we were no longer short of suspects, at any rate. I looked up to see Aunt Agnes waving her hand at me.

"Let's look for Gorgona's altar room."

I frowned. "Do you think there will be incriminating evidence about The Other in there?"

Aunt Agnes paused, her hand to her chin. "The very fact that Gorgona made us executors leads me to believe she kept all incriminating evidence elsewhere. Sure, she didn't expect to be murdered, but still…" Aunt Agnes pulled a potion from her handbag. "I'm sure the room will be protected by very nasty spells and hexes."

We found the altar room at the end of a long corridor. Aunt Agnes pointed to the pulsating golden symbols covering the door. "I don't like the look of this, not at all. I'll deal with it, and the rest of you put all the paperwork you can find into boxes. Quick, we have to work fast."

Aunt Maude, Aunt Dorothy, and I worked feverishly, putting all the documents we could find into boxes. There were plenty of bedrooms in the house, as well as the study, and the huge safe in the garage. We had only just stuffed the last box into the truck when Jezabeth drove up behind us.

"Perfect timing," Aunt Agnes said with a sigh of relief.

"Did you make a copy of the key for Hemlock?" Jezabeth demanded by way of greeting.

Agnes handed the key to her. She took without thanking her and looked around for her daughter who was just getting out of the car. Hemlock took a cigarette out of her mouth and threw it into the gutter before stomping on it. I figured it contained more than nicotine. Hemlock sauntered over to us. "What are you doing here?" she snapped. "You're not a beneficiary!"

"I'm helping," I countered.

She shot me a malicious look. I thought she looked like a Pekinese dog. I quite liked Pekinese dogs, but it wasn't a look that sat well on a human face. Her bottom lip jutted out in a petulant fashion.

"Well, I've gotta move into my house now. Catch youse later."

She trudged up the front stairs.

"We haven't finished inside yet," Aunt Agnes called after her.

Jezabeth swung around towards Agnes, her hands on her hips. "You haven't finished yet? What have you been doing all morning?" Her eyes narrowed with nastiness. "You've made poor Hemlock upset. You're making her feel like an unwelcome houseguest."

"She *is* an unwelcome houseguest," I muttered, but Aunt Agnes elbowed me.

"Jezabeth, might I remind you that the will did not mention anybody staying in the house. If Hemlock is to stay in the house, she will have to abide by our rules. She can't smoke or consume any illegal substances while in the house, and she will have to obey the law."

Jezabeth waved one hand at Agnes in dismissal. "Of course, of course. You wouldn't get a nicer person than dear Hemlock. She is always thinking of others. Why, look what she's done for you over the years!"

"What *has* she done for me over the years?" Aunt Agnes said, clearly confused.

Jezabeth looked off into the distance and bit her lip. Finally, she said, "Lots of things. Well, come inside if you must. I hope you won't be here for long."

We all followed her inside. I thought she would object to me going into the house, but she didn't. "What have you taken out of the house?" she asked Agnes, her tone full of suspicion.

"Only legal documents," Aunt Agnes said as quick as a flash.

"Did you take the jewellery?"

Aunt Agnes shook her head.

Jezabeth turned to her daughter. "Quick, Hemlock, look through your grandmother's clothes. Sometimes, she had jewellery in her pockets."

"Any jewellery has to be given to us so we can sort through it under the terms of the will," Agnes said.

A cunning look passed over Jezabeth's face. "Yes, of course, of course," she said with a big wink at Hemlock. "Off you go, Hemlock."

Hemlock shot us a nasty look. She looked just as much of a troll as her grandmother. As she walked away, I heard her mutter to herself, "There's bad energy here. This house needs a lot of incense."

I had never met a more infuriating person in my life. "Go with Hemlock, Dorothy," Agnes said. "Make sure that she brings any jewellery that she finds out here. In fact, that's what we should all do now, find all the jewellery and bring it to the kitchen table."

I went back into the study to search for jewellery. I found two heavy gold bracelets and one teeny gold bracelet which I thought might be fake. That was the only jewellery I found, so I took it back to the kitchen. I didn't know what else to do, so I waited for the others to appear.

When they didn't turn up, I thought I'd look through the kitchen cupboards just in case there was jewellery hidden in there. I didn't find any, but amongst numerous packets of coffee and bottles of caramel syrup, I did find tins of cat food. I went in search of Aunt Agnes and found her in one of the bedrooms, looking through a chest of drawers. "There's cat food in the kitchen cupboards," I announced.

Aunt Agnes looked up in surprise. "I thought Gorgona didn't like pets."

I shook my head. "Remember, she said Ethelbert hated pets, but she liked them."

Aunt Agnes tapped her chin with one finger.

"No, if I remember correctly, she said she liked pets but said they were too much expense."

"Then why is there cat food in her cupboards?" I said. "I hope there isn't some poor kitty in the house. She'd have to be hungry by now, maybe thirsty too."

"Then we have to look for a cat," Agnes said. "Did you see a litter box?"

I shook my head. "Good thinking! I'll go and look now."

As I walked out of the room, I looked over my shoulder. "Or maybe she was an outside cat."

By now, Agnes had her head in a drawer, so I went back to the kitchen. I looked in the laundry room for a litter box but didn't find one. There was a key in the back door, so I let myself into the back yard. It was a tiny yard, with layers of rock work, and the particularly large house behind it overlooked most of the yard. Jasmine, growing wild, covered most of the rocks and gave off the most delightful fragrance.

"Here kitty, kitty," I called out. I looked everywhere but could see no cat. There were no food or water bowls set out anywhere. I walked back and reported this to Aunt Agnes.

"It seems she didn't have a cat then," Agnes said. "I wonder why she had the cat food?"

I shrugged. "She had cans of cat food and two packets of dried cat food as well as a few packets of cat treats."

"That *is* awfully strange," Agnes admitted.

Just then, Jezabeth called us loudly, telling us to go to the kitchen. We hurried to the kitchen to find the others gathered there. In the middle of the table was a huge pile of jewellery.

"Did your mother own a cat?" I asked Jezabeth.

She narrowed her eyes. "Not as far as I know. Why?"

"There are cans of cat food in the cupboards."

"Are there now!" Jezabeth's eyes glittered. "Have they been there a long time?"

"Well, I didn't check the use by date," I said, somewhat puzzled by her intense interest. "If there's a cat, we will have to find it. The poor thing is probably hungry by now."

"Now, I have something important to say," Aunt Agnes began. "Jezabeth, I know we mentioned this briefly to you before, but my sisters and I are firmly convinced that your mother was murdered. The police say it was natural circumstances, but let's face facts—it's clear she was murdered. Do you want to avenge your mother's death? Or at least find out who murdered her?"

Hemlock burst into floods of tears. Or rather, she was making sobbing sounds, but I couldn't see any tears coming from her eyes. "How could you say such a thing?" she cried. "No one wanted to murder my grannie! She was so nice."

I stared at her in shock. Maybe we were thinking of different people.

Hemlock pushed on. "Everybody loved her!"

Jezabeth patted Hemlock on the back rather too hard. "Hush, Hemlock," she snapped. "Get a grip." To Agnes, she said, "Can't you stop creating all this drama? You've upset Hemlock. No one likes drama but you, Agnes, and you're always causing it. Hemlock is very sensitive to drama. She will get a bout of anxiety with all this drama in the room."

"Back to the question of your mother's murder," Agnes began, but Jezabeth cut her off.

"My mother wasn't murdered!" she yelled at the top of her lungs. "She wasn't murdered, I tell you! And don't you dare suggest to the police that she was murdered, because probate won't be able to go ahead if you do."

I wondered why Jezabeth was protesting so much. Had she, in fact, murdered her mother, or did she simply want to get her inheritance as soon as possible? I knew in the state of New South Wales that probate could drag on for many months, and if Jezabeth had fallen on hard times, she would want the money as soon as possible.

"Anyway, let's forget all this talk about my mother's death by *natural causes* and let's turn our attention to the jewellery."

"We will take the jewellery with us and divide it up later, according to the terms of the will," Agnes said.

"Not so fast," Jezabeth said, her eyes glittering with something that could only be greed. "I gave my mother this diamond necklace, so I'm taking it back." Her hand moved out and snatched the diamond necklace almost faster than the eye could see.

"And my mother promised this heavy gold chain to my dear daughter, Hemlock," Jezabeth continued. She greedily snatched the thick gold chain.

"But, but each piece would be worth over ten thousand dollars," Aunt Agnes sputtered.

Jezabeth narrowed her eyes. "What of it?"

"We will deal with all the jewellery later," Agnes said, shoving it all into a box before Jezabeth could get her greedy clutches on any more of it. "Now, you choose a room, Hemlock. The rooms are all clean and tidy. Don't go into the other bedrooms while you're here, so we can make sure they stay nice and clean for sale."

Hemlock jutted out her bottom lip and pouted. "Sure, whatever. I'll have my grandmother's room, the one with the big en-suite bathroom."

Aunt Agnes rubbed her forehead. "Fine. Try to stay out of the other rooms as much as you can."

"Why are you upsetting Hemlock like this?" Jezabeth said. "The poor girl has come all this way from Adelaide and you're making her feel unwelcome in her own grandmother's house. Hemlock can have the run of the house and do whatever she likes."

Aunt Agnes stood up and drew herself up to her full height, looming over Jezabeth. "No, I'm afraid she cannot. This is not her house and it's not your house." Jezabeth made to protest, but Agnes held up one hand, palm outwards. "You are to receive a share of the house, but Hemlock isn't. My sisters and I are executors of the will and you will have to do what we say. Otherwise, probate won't be able to proceed and it will take you a lot longer to get any money."

Hemlock burst into another bout of fake tears. "Youse are awful," she screamed at the top of her lungs. Her cheeks puffed up like cane toad's and her eyes turned bloodshot. "Why can't you have any compassion for me? I can't handle all this drama!" She waved her arms around like a windmill and ran out of the room. I noticed her pockets were bulging and I figured she'd stolen some jewellery when Aunt Dorothy wasn't looking.

I fervently hoped I never had to be an executor of a will, not when relatives could be as malevolent as this.

CHAPTER 9

I was sitting in the funeral director's office along with the aunts, Jezabeth, and Hemlock. The aunts had persuaded me to come along. Aunt Agnes had told Jezabeth that the executors had to attend to make sure the funeral was in accordance with the instructions of the will.

After the funeral consultant lady had introduced herself and shaken our hands, she indicated we should sit opposite her at a white table. Everything in the room was white. Hemlock was seated next to a bowl of white mints. She took a handful and shoved some in her mouth and the rest in her pocket.

"Now, have you brought the clothes you wish

your mother to be buried in?" the consultant asked Jezabeth.

"No. It's not an open casket, so what does it matter what she's buried in? Nobody is going to peek in and look at her."

The consultant was visibly shocked.

"But wouldn't you like an open casket?" asked Aunt Agnes.

"No!" Jezabeth snapped.

"I don't think it costs any more," Aunt Agnes said, "but if it does, I'm happy to pay the extra."

The consultant attempted a smile. "Now, we didn't have a chance to discuss this on the phone. Who is the minister who will be taking the service?"

"There won't be a service," Jezabeth said. "There will just be a burial. In the ground," she added for good measure.

The consultant's eyes shot skyward. "No service?" she repeated.

"That's right," Jezabeth said. "No service. And she is to be cremated."

"No, she can't be cremated under the terms of her will," Aunt Agnes said. "She left specific instructions that she wasn't to be cremated."

"All this drama!" Hemlock said. "Just cremate

Grannie, for goodness sake, Aunt Agnes. Honestly, it's beyond me why you create all this drama."

Aunt Agnes turned to her. "It was your grandmother herself who asked not to be cremated."

The consultant spoke up. "Well, she can't be cremated if her will expressly asked that she not be," she said, I thought rather bravely.

Jezabeth fixed her with a steely glare. "All right then, but there won't be a minister. We will simply bury her."

"Will there be a service at the cemetery?" the consultant asked.

Jezabeth pointed to Aunt Agnes. "Ask her! She's got all the answers."

"Your mother simply asked that she not be cremated, that's all," Aunt Agnes said in even tones. "And my sisters and I would like it to be an open casket, but you have flatly refused."

Jezabeth did not respond, but Hemlock muttered to herself.

"So, which cemetery would you like?" the consultant asked, before reeling off a list of cemeteries.

"One in Lighthouse Bay," Jezabeth said.

"There are several," she said, naming them.

As soon as she stopped, Jezabeth said, "That one."

"Which one?"

"The last one that you said."

"So, when would you like to see it?"

Jezabeth looked affronted. "See it? Why would I want to see it?"

The consultant appeared rather surprised. "Well, I assume, to see if it's nice. The cemetery you have chosen has nice flowerbeds all around. It's quite pretty."

"I doubt my mother would care," Jezabeth said in steely tones. "She's dead. How soon can we have the funeral?"

The consultant pushed a brochure across the table. "I'll leave the room and call the cemetery. Meanwhile, you can look at the brochure. It has the prices listed at the bottom." She tapped one fingernail on the brochure.

"This is quite expensive," Jezabeth complained. "It would have been much better to have had her cremated."

No one responded. We could all hear the consultant speaking on the phone in the next room, explaining to the cemetery that the relatives did not want to see the gravesite first.

She came back into the room. "We can book you in for the day after tomorrow, if that would suit," she said. "It just depends whether there is an available coffin."

Jezabeth sighed. "Which coffins *are* available?"

The consultant opened another glossy brochure. "We have these nice wooden ones and then there are also some new environmental coffins made out of cardboard."

Jezabeth's eyes lit up. "Cardboard? That sounds perfect. Yes, we can bury her in a cardboard coffin." She eagerly thumbed through the brochure before letting out a shriek. "What? These cardboard ones are as expensive as normal coffins."

"Yes, they are a little more expensive than the lower-priced range of coffins, and they take a week to make, maybe longer," the consultant said.

Jezabeth was clearly in a temper. "All right, so what's the cheapest coffin you actually have in stock right now, as of this minute?"

"I'll have to go out and make a few calls to find out," the consultant said.

"You do that," Jezabeth spat.

The consultant soon returned and showed Jezabeth a photo. I noticed all the mints had disappeared, and Hemlock was chewing. "We have this coffin in stock, and it's in the lower price range. Your mother could be buried in this coffin the day after tomorrow."

"It's a deal," Jezabeth said, "unless you have any further objections, Agnes?"

"That's fine," Agnes said.

"Now, do you want the coffin to be placed above the ground? For the service at the cemetery, a minister usually talks and then someone gives me a subtle nod and I press the button to lower the coffin," she said.

"But we've already told you there won't be a minister," Jezabeth yelled.

"Well, how would you like to have the service?" the consultant asked. I wondered if she'd ever had anyone as difficult as Jezabeth before. I figured not.

"I don't know. Would you like to say anything at the gravesite, Hemlock?"

"Yes, I'd like to say something and I'd like to place some roses on top of Grannie's coffin," Hemlock said.

"Okay, then we don't want you to lower the coffin while we're there. Poor Hemlock will be too upset seeing the coffin lowered. We'll say something and then after we leave, you can lower the coffin."

The consultant left the room for a few minutes.

She didn't give a reason this time. I wondered if she had left to have a stiff shot of gin. Goodness knows she would have needed one. When she returned, Jezabeth had to sign a lot of paperwork, as did the aunts.

"The death certificate will be mailed to one of you," the consultant said. "Who should I send it to?"

"You can send it to me," Jezabeth said. "You have my address."

The consultant scrawled something on a piece of paper.

"Since it isn't an open casket, do you mind if we see Gorgona, I mean Euphemia, before the funeral?" Aunt Agnes asked.

Jezabeth waved one long, bony finger at her. "Do whatever you like, so long as it doesn't cost anything."

"Then is it possible to see her?" Agnes asked the consultant.

"Well, let us put some make-up on her first," the consultant said. "Could you do that on the morning of the funeral? We're not prepared for you to see her today. It takes time."

"I don't want you to see Grannie," Hemlock said firmly. "I know Grannie doesn't want you to see her like that. Grannie wants everybody to remember her how she was."

"We were her cousins and we want to say goodbye to her," Aunt Agnes said firmly.

"I don't want you to and I'm her granddaughter," Hemlock said. She burst into another bout of fake tears.

"Can't you see you're upsetting Hemlock?" Jezabeth said tersely. "Poor Hemlock! She's sensitive, and she doesn't want you to see her grandmother."

"Nobody is gonna look at Grannie!" Hemlock screamed.

"I understand you might not want to look at your grandmother, but we, her cousins, would like to say our last goodbyes," Aunt Agnes said calmly. "Jezabeth, please grant us our dearest wish by letting us see your mother."

"No!" Jezabeth snapped.

I raised my eyebrows. So much for Aunt Agnes's plan to have an open casket or a viewing. Now we were going to have to find another way to procure Gorgona's hair to have it tested for poison.

"But we want to see our cousin," Aunt Maude said. "Cousins outdo granddaughters."

"This isn't a card game," Jezabeth snapped.

"I'm her daughter and I won't allow you to see her."

"Well, I'm an executor and I want to see her," Aunt Maude said.

"Why don't you all discuss it outside?" the consultant said. "I don't want to hurry you out, but I have other clients arriving at any minute. It was lovely to meet you all. I'll see you again the day after tomorrow." With that, she ushered us out of the office.

Aunt Agnes stayed back. "Where do you keep the body?"

The consultant looked surprised. "The body?" she echoed.

"Yes, where is the body of Euphemia Jones now? I assume it's not on the premises."

The consultant shook her head. "Oh no, we're taking good care of her."

"Yes, but exactly *where* is she?"

"Oh, she's at our head office morgue."

"In Lighthouse Bay?"

The consultant nodded.

"Thanks," Aunt Agnes said.

As we walked out, we saw Hemlock sitting on the side of the road, her head between her knees.

Jezabeth marched over to us. "Look what you've

done!" she yelled at Aunt Agnes. "You've given Hemlock an anxiety attack by wanting to see her grandmother. She told you she didn't want you to, but you kept insisting. How can you be so nasty? You've upset Hemlock." With that, she marched away to her car, leaving Hemlock sitting on the side of the road.

"Your plans to see Gorgona nearly worked out," I said to Aunt Agnes. "What a pity Hemlock objected."

"I'll have to drive past the morgue and see if we can break in," Aunt Agnes said. "Then we can take some of her hair."

"I have an idea," Aunt Dorothy said. "We could swap the bodies. I saw it on a TV show. They thought they shot someone who was a spy, but the spy set it all up. She had someone else's body in the bushes and she swapped places with them. If we swap the body, then we can take as many samples of Gorgona's hair as we want."

"Have you completely lost your mind, Dorothy?" Aunt Agnes said, while Aunt Maude chuckled.

Aunt Dorothy looked affronted. "I thought it was an excellent idea. If we can't get some of her hair, then we can swap her body for someone else's, take her home to the manor and take lots of hair samples there."

Aunt Agnes groaned. "Honestly, Dorothy! Sometimes I wonder about you. If we couldn't take some of her hair, then how would we be able to take her whole body?"

Aunt Dorothy looked crestfallen. "I hadn't thought of that."

"I'll drive past the morgue now," Agnes said. "What's the address again?"

I consulted my notes. "It's 199 Flinders Drive."

"Did you say 199 Flinders Drive?" Maude said. "That's where Pillsbury works! He's a cosmetician."

CHAPTER 10

*L*inda and I were sitting at a local café with the aunts, staring at the DVD cover of Karen and the mystery man. "We really can't see his face," Linda said, peering at the photo.

When the waitress approached, Maude snatched the DVD cover from her and turned it upside down. After we gave our orders for coffee and cake, Maude flipped the cover up. She tapped her chin. "What if we take the photo home and scan it, then take it to a photo studio and have it blown up?"

Aunt Agnes pulled her reading glasses out of her handbag and took the DVD case from Maude. She turned the case this way and that. "I don't think there's enough of his face to see, no matter how much it's blown up. You can only see the corner of his mouth and the edge of one eye. You can't even see his nose, and a sheet is covering the top of his head."

"Could we pressure Karen into telling us who he is?" I suggested.

The aunts shook their heads. "Well, maybe as a last resort," Aunt Agnes conceded, "but she's hardly likely to give us the information, considering she was no doubt being blackmailed over it. She wants to keep that secret at all costs, especially if she murdered Gorgona."

"Then if Karen won't tell us, who can?" I asked.

Aunt Agnes slapped the DVD cover down on the table hard, making us all jump. "I know! Killian Cosgrove wouldn't have known, but Mrs Mumbles might have."

"Why would she have known?" I said.

"Mrs Mumbles is a clever woman," Aunt Agnes said. "She was having an affair with Killian, and given that she seemed to be insanely jealous, I bet she kept a close eye on Karen. If anyone is going to know who Karen was having an affair with, then it would be Mrs Mumbles."

"I think it's an awful stretch, Agnes," Aunt Maude said. "It's a long shot."

Aunt Agnes shrugged. "Maybe, but can you think of any alternatives?"

We all shook our heads.

"But even if Mrs Mumbles does know the identity of the mystery man, why would she tell you?" Linda asked.

Aunt Agnes narrowed her eyes. "You do have a good point, Linda." She was silent for a moment before saying, adding, "You know, that's the angle we can take."

I was puzzled. "What angle?"

"The angle that Mrs Mumbles probably hated Karen. After all, she was clearly in love with Killian Cosgrove and he didn't leave his wife for her."

"But he…" I began, but she interrupted me.

"Whatever the reason, Valkyrie, the fact remains that he didn't leave his wife for Mrs Mumbles and so she probably resented Karen, hated her even. She might be only too pleased to tell us who Karen was seeing."

"That might be true," I countered, "but she won't be happy with us, given we're the reason that she's in jail right now on remand without bail, awaiting trial."

"We can only try," Aunt Agnes said. "What can it hurt?"

"I assume she's in a Sydney prison, so it would involve booking in for a visit and having to go to Sydney," Maude said. "That's a waste of a whole day."

"It isn't a waste of a day if we get something out of her," Agnes countered.

"Is there anybody else who would know who Karen is seeing?" Linda said. "I know! Why don't we follow her?"

"That's a fantastic idea," Aunt Agnes said, just as the waitress appeared with the coffee.

"Will you be bringing our cakes soon please?" asked Aunt Maude. "We would like our cakes with our coffee."

The waitress apologised and went to fetch our cakes.

"We should split up on this one," Aunt Agnes said. "Valkyrie, why don't you and Linda tail Karen? Maude, keep an eye on Cary and things at the manor, while Dorothy and I will go and see Mrs Mumbles."

"Sure," I said. "When do you plan to do this?"

"We will book in for the soonest appointment," Agnes said. "Valkyrie, do you have your iPad on you?" I nodded. She pushed on. "Make me a list of prisons in Sydney where women are held on remand, and I'll call them all and try to track down Mrs Mumbles."

"What if she refuses to see you?" I asked.

She shrugged. "Well, then we won't go, but I imagine she would be bored in prison and would be at least curious as to why we want to visit."

"Maybe." I was unconvinced.

And so, an hour later, Linda and I found ourselves sitting in a café not far from Killian and Karen's nail salon in a major shopping centre.

This time, we had both ordered decaf coffee as our caffeine levels were through the roof.

"I wish we could see inside the salon from here," Linda lamented.

"We can see who comes and goes," I pointed out.

"And it's good that it's a major shopping centre and there is no back way out," Linda said. "We'll be able to see Karen when she leaves."

"What if her lover lives somewhere else and only comes to town once a month or something?"

Linda sighed. "I hadn't thought of that. This could turn out to be quite boring. Would you like some cake?"

I clutched my stomach. "No, I couldn't eat another thing."

"When I rang up to pretend to book an appointment with Karen earlier, they said she was only available until noon and after that I'd have to book with some other woman," Linda said. "I made an excuse, of course. I wonder if it's worth booking in for a pedicure, and cross-examining those other women. They might have a clue about who she's seeing."

I disagreed. "I don't think so. Don't forget, Karen jointly owns the salon along with her husband. Sure, he's in prison now, but she would have been careful for ages to make sure no one from the salon knew that she was having an affair."

"You're right." Linda turned over her phone on the table and looked at the time. "It's noon now, and there's no sign of her."

"She's probably instructing the staff or something," I said, before grabbing Linda's arm. "Look, here she comes now."

Karen Cosgrove walked out of the salon and headed in our direction. I took a menu from the table and stuck my head behind it. Linda did the same. "She just passed us," I said, peeking around the menu. "She's going into the supermarket."

"She has to come back past us," Linda said. "We don't have to move."

Karen was only in the supermarket for five or so minutes before she came out. "Get ready," I said to Linda. "Oh, wait! She's gone to the health food shop."

Karen was in the health food shop for a further five minutes. "Here she comes now," I said.

Linda rolled her eyes. "I hope she leaves now. This is going to be boring if she goes into every single shop."

"Okay, she's heading away. Let's go." I stood up.

Karen headed away from the shops and down the escalators to the car park. Linda and I kept our distance, but there were plenty of shoppers around us to hide us.

"Okay, she's going to her car. It seems to be in the general direction of my car," Linda said.

I nodded to the far exit diagonally opposite us. "I think she'll leave that way."

I got in Linda's car. She reversed and then drove off slowly in the direction of Karen's car. She followed her, taking care not to get too close.

"I googled her home address and it looks like she's headed there now," I said with disappointment.

"Maybe she'll stay there all afternoon and the boyfriend won't visit," Linda said.

I pulled a face. "And I doubt he could go to her house anyway, because his car would be seen outside. I think this is a wild goose chase."

We drove along to the outskirts of town. Although I had heard of the street in which she lived, I didn't realise it was a new development with hardly any houses around. Hers was the only house built in her cul-de-sac and all the others were under construction.

"That's convenient if the boyfriend wants to visit her," Linda said as she parked down the road and we watched Karen's car drive into her garage.

"I've been thinking about it," I said. "She would have had a routine with her lover. Obviously, he wouldn't have gone to her house because of her husband, Killian. That means Karen would have had to go elsewhere to visit her lover."

"That's true!" Linda exclaimed. "And since he was married, then they couldn't meet at his house either. They must've met at a motel."

"And at a motel where nobody knew them," I said. "Clearly, Karen didn't want news of her affair getting back to Killian, so I'd be surprised if they met in a motel in Lighthouse Bay."

"But since Karen was married and ran a business, she wouldn't have been able to get away often."

I turned to Linda. "What do you mean?"

"I mean, Karen was married and ran a business in Lighthouse Bay with her husband. That means she would have been very careful with her absences, or her husband would have known something was going on."

"But her husband was having an affair with Mrs Mumbles," I said. "He must have had unexplained absences."

"Then that's when Karen had her opportunity," Linda said, "but my point is, she must have been having an affair with someone who lives in town."

"That's true," I said. "And we have established that they couldn't have met at her house. Maybe, it's someone from the same shopping centre, and then no one would be any the wiser."

Linda readily agreed. "I think it must be something like that. You know, Killian Cosgrove used to go to those orchid club meetings, so that's when Karen would have had plenty of time to get up to no good."

I clutched my head with both hands. "This is doing my head in! I doubt we will ever figure this one out. I think we've come to a dead end. And we might as well leave, because we can't sit outside her house all day, hoping this person will show up."

Linda opened her mouth to say something, when Aunt Agnes called me. I swiped my screen.

"I know who the mystery man in the photo is!" Agnes exclaimed.

CHAPTER 11

"*W*ho was it?" I asked.

"Franklyn Sutton!"

Linda and I exchanged glances. Just then, my phone cut out. I pressed the button to call Aunt Agnes back, but it went straight to voicemail. "Have you ever heard of Franklyn Sutton?" I asked Linda.

She nodded. "The name does sound a bit familiar, and your aunt said it as if she expected us to know who it was."

Just then, my phone rang again. "The phone cut out," Aunt Agnes said, stating the obvious.

"Who is Franklyn Sutton?" I asked her.

"He's a town councillor."

Linda and I looked at each other and nodded.

"That's right. I saw him on TV the other week," I said.

"He's on TV all the time. He has political aspirations."

"He's already on the town council," I pointed out.

Aunt Agnes made a sound of dismissal. "No, Valkyrie, I mean political aspirations in the sense of *Federal* politics. Anyway, he's always on TV going on about family values. In fact, that's his platform—strong morals and family values. It wouldn't do if it got out that he'd been having an affair with Karen Cosgrove. His wife's on a lot of charity boards. It wouldn't go down at all well."

"How did you find out it was him?" I asked her.

"We actually found the DVD, and we watched it."

"You watched the sex tape?" Linda asked with a giggle.

"Yes, I did," Aunt Agnes said. "I thought I'd seen everything, but that tape was something else! He would be *most* upset if it was leaked to the press."

"Then it makes more sense if he was the killer," I said. "Out of everybody, he had the most to lose."

"As far as we know," Aunt Agnes said. "There

could be people with other motives and we just don't know about them yet."

I nodded, and then realised she couldn't see me. "Fair enough, but it kind of absolves Karen."

"Why do you say that?" Linda asked me.

"Why would Karen want to murder the blackmailer now? Her husband is already out of the way in prison awaiting trial, and it's her lover who would be implicated."

"Maybe she doesn't want her lover implicated, and maybe she took matters into her own hands," Agnes said.

I rubbed my forehead. "Yes, of course, you're right. I haven't been sleeping well since Lucas has been away, and it must be affecting my thinking. Anyway, we don't have to stake out Karen anymore, do we?" I asked hopefully.

"No," Aunt Agnes said. "If Linda wouldn't mind taking you back to the shopping centre, I think Dorothy, Maude, you, and I should pay a little visit to Franklyn Sutton."

"What? Actually visit him in his office?"

"Yes."

I was surprised. "What do you plan to say to him?"

"I don't have any plans. I'm going to wing it." With that, she hung up.

"That doesn't sound good to me," I said to Linda, who had already started the engine and was turning the car around. "If he's the murderer, then he might come after us if he knows we've got evidence against him."

I repeated the sentiments to Aunt Agnes after Linda left me at the shopping centre, but she remained unmoved. "He can't murder the four of us," she said.

"Why not?" I said with a shrug.

Aunt Agnes patted my shoulder. "Don't worry about it."

"Don't we need an appointment or something?" I said, hoping we would so I could avoid seeing him.

"We'll try to get in now," she said.

The other aunts were in agreement with her, so I had no choice but to follow. There was no receptionist at the front desk in the tiny office. I noted it wasn't far from Karen Cosgrove's nail salon and was down a corridor that led to a wall cupboards, which I assumed were full of cleaning implements. Aunt Agnes ran a bell on the desk.

A man stepped out. I recognised him at once as Franklyn Sutton. He was tall and well built, and wearing a sickly smile and an ill-fitting suit. "Hello, ladies. What can I do for you?"

Aunt Agnes shot him a wide smile. "I wonder if you could spare us a few minutes of your time? Your receptionist doesn't appear to be here."

"Oh, she's not full-time," he said. "Sure, I'm happy to help my constituents. Please come through to my office." He nodded at each one of us in turn.

We walked into his office. There were only three chairs opposite his desk, so he popped back out and returned with a chair from the tiny waiting room.

The office was entirely depressing, painted a shade somewhere between dirty cream and murky grey. There was a window, but it was small and didn't afford much light even with the curtains opened as he had them now. Several cream filing cabinets sat around the room and perched on top of the one in the corner was a dead potted plant.

"Terrible fires we've had lately," he said.

Aunt Agnes agreed. "Yes. Hopefully, we'll have some rain soon and it will clear the air. The smoke is coming from south of Taree."

The man smiled again. "Well, what can I do for you ladies? Are you here to complain about the Prime Minister?" He leant across the desk and gave us a huge wink. "I have to support him, of course, but…" He let his voice trail away and winked again.

"My name is Agnes Jasper, and these are my sisters, Dorothy and Maude. This is our niece, Valkyrie."

"Pepper," I said automatically.

"We own the Mugwort Manor Bed and Breakfast."

I noticed a flicker of recognition cross his face, followed by something else—maybe alarm?

"We had a boarder, Ethelbert Jones, was murdered on our premises not too long ago."

He nodded slowly. "Oh yes, a terrible business." He shook his head. "A terrible business."

"And his wife died the other day. Her name was Euphemia."

He looked shocked. "Euphemia is dead?"

Aunt Agnes nodded. "Did you know her?"

He almost fell over himself saying he didn't. "No, no, no. I had heard of her, of course, because her husband was murdered and it made the news. I have to know about these things, you see. But I've never met her." Gone was his false charm, to be replaced by tension.

"The police said it was natural causes," Aunt Agnes continued.

He nodded. "Yes, very sad. Maybe the stress of her husband's murder took its toll on her."

Aunt Agnes shook her head. "To the contrary, we are convinced she was murdered."

"Murdered?" he repeated. "But didn't you just say the police said it was natural causes?"

"The police didn't do a post-mortem or even take toxicology samples," Aunt Agnes said. "They didn't see a bullet wound or a stab wound, so they assumed it was natural causes. It was the wrong assumption, of course."

"I don't see how I can help you," he said slowly. "Do you want me to speak to the police and ask them to open a case?"

Aunt Agnes did not answer his question, but said, "It was well known that her husband, Ethelbert, was murdered because he was blackmailing Killian Cosgrove and Mrs Mumbles." She looked at him for a response, but there wasn't one. She pushed on. "And so we think that another blackmail victim murdered Euphemia."

"I'm sorry, but I don't think I'm following you," Sutton said in clipped tones.

"Why don't I come straight to the point?" Aunt Agnes said.

He leant back in his chair. "Please do."

Aunt Agnes took the DVD case from her handbag and pushed it across the table to him. "Well then, to come straight to the point, we are asking you if you murdered Euphemia Jones."

He picked up the DVD case, looked at it, and dropped it like a hot potato. "Who are those people?" he said, his eyes darting wildly from side to side.

"We know it's you," Aunt Agnes said. "We watched the sex tape."

Sutton's hand flew to his throat. "You did?" he squeaked. "What do you want from me?"

Aunt Maude spoke for the first time. "We don't want to blackmail you or anything like that, if that's what you're thinking. We just want to know whether you murdered Euphemia."

Sutton landed his chair with a thud. "Of course, I didn't murder her! This can't get out. If my wife found out…" His voice trailed away. I noticed his hands were shaking.

"We're not going to tell your wife or tell the police, unless we find out you were the one who murdered Euphemia," Agnes said.

"You're not going to blackmail me?"

The aunts shook their heads.

"You're not going to tell my wife? Or tell the police?"

Aunt Agnes leant across the desk and drummed her fingers on the mouse pad sitting opposite her. "Listen, we're not going to tell anybody, but you have to convince us you didn't murder Euphemia Jones. Do you have an alibi?"

"When did she die?" he asked.

"Four days ago," Aunt Maude said.

He looked up at the ceiling. "I wasn't in town that day."

"Where were you?" Agnes asked him.

"I drove to Newcastle and back that day. I had a political meeting there."

"What time did the meeting start?"

"It started at nine, and went all morning."

Aunt Agnes took out a notepad and wrote it down. "I see. Thanks for your help."

He reached for the DVD, but Aunt Agnes snatched it. "We won't tell anyone; you can rest assured of that, but we *are* keeping it for insurance. We've made several copies and we have given them to our lawyers in case anything were to happen to us."

"I'm not a murderer," he squeaked.

"Let's hope so." With that, Aunt Agnes stood up. We all stood up and followed her out.

When we were back in the hallway, Aunt Maude asked, "What do you make of that?"

"We'll have to check out his alibi," Aunt Agnes said, "but I doubt it will be at all revealing."

"Why not?" Dorothy asked her.

"His alibi simply means he was in Newcastle at the time Gorgona died, which means he couldn't have injected her with poison on that day. It's possible she was poisoned by something in the cottage that she had eaten the day before, for all we know. Maybe, she had been eating the poisoned substance over a period of days. In fact, he could have visited her the day before and he could have given her a poisonous substance. I'm afraid alibis aren't much help when we don't know when the poison was administered or even what it was."

"It will take a week to get the results back from the lab. However, Pillsbury will be back at the morgue this afternoon," Dorothy said. "Is the plan still to get some of Gorgona's hair?"

"Yes, and there's a lab in Lismore," Aunt Agnes said. "We will send it by express post, and it will arrive tomorrow, but that lab too can take up to a week to process samples. It tests for arsenic but no other poisons."

"If it wasn't arsenic or one of the substances the other labs test for, then how do we find out what the poison was?" I asked her.

We all looked at each other in silence. Our investigation wasn't going at all well.

CHAPTER 12

We drove to the morgue on the other side of town. "I didn't know Pillsbury was a cosmetician," I said to Aunt Maude.

"Yes, he works for that funeral company that Jezabeth is using for her mother's funeral," Maude said, although of course we all knew that already. "I didn't put two and two together at first."

"How many morgues are there in this town?" I asked.

"The hospitals have them, of course, but Pillsbury told me that there are a few smaller, privately owned ones owned by the funeral companies in town. They're basically just freezer rooms—nothing fancy."

"I wouldn't think that could be a full-time job for Pillsbury," Aunt Agnes said.

"I have no idea," Aunt Maude said with a shrug. "I don't really care, to be honest. I just thought he'd make a good sugar daddy."

Aunt Agnes and Aunt Dorothy exchanged glances. I thought it best not to comment. Aunt Agnes stopped the car opposite a small, pale green building at a crossroads. We were about to get out of the car when Aunt Agnes screeched, "Freeze!" followed by, in more measured tones, "Quick! Get back in the car."

We all did as she asked. "Look, Hemlock and Jezabeth have just come out."

"Wow, that was lucky," I said. "Imagine if they had caught us in there."

"More to the point, what were they doing in there?" Agnes said.

"I suppose we'll find out soon enough."

"Duck!" Agnes said.

We all ducked. "My legs are cramped! When can I stick my head up?" Dorothy asked after an interval.

"Hush," Aunt Agnes hissed. "I'll take a little peek." She raised her head a little and then ducked back. "Just give it another minute or so. They're getting in a car now."

After Dorothy complained again, Agnes looked once more. "The coast is clear," she said with a sigh of relief. "They've gone."

"Do you think they saw us?" Maude asked.

"I don't think so," Agnes said. "They're both too self-absorbed to notice anything much apart from themselves."

We crossed the road and hurried into the big green building which also housed a lawyer's office and a dentist. I shuddered as I walked past the dentist. Maude opened the door to the little morgue and ushered us inside.

Pillsbury was standing there, looking at his clipboard. He looked up and smiled when he saw Maude. "Oh, it's lovely to see you all," he said although he addressed that comment to Maude.

Maude came straight to the point. "We just saw our cousin, Jezabeth, come in here with her daughter. What did they want?"

"They came in here to make sure Euphemia Jones could not be viewed by anyone." His face fell. "I'm afraid they specifically mentioned you, Maude, and your lovely sisters."

"Our cousin isn't exactly a nice woman," Maude said.

Pillsbury nodded slowly. "So, is this just a social call?"

Aunt Agnes stepped forward. She took a deep breath, and then said, "Dorothy, Maude, and I believe Euphemia Jones was murdered. The police were dismissive and said it was natural causes, but we are certain she was poisoned."

Pillsbury looked shocked. "Poisoned, you say?"

Aunt Agnes nodded solemnly. "We came here to sneak a piece of her hair so we could send it away for sampling to prove she had been poisoned."

"But hair doesn't test for many poisons," Pillsbury said. "You'd be much better off with a toxicology report."

"And how do we get one of those done?" Agnes asked him.

He looked over the top of his glasses. "I don't think you can. Not unless you're a police officer or the like."

"Precisely. That's why we need to take a hair sample. I know it doesn't test for all the poisons, but at least we could discount arsenic."

Pillsbury tapped his chin. "Arsenic. What were her symptoms?"

"She complained of feeling very ill and said she had terrible stomach pains."

"That was it?" Pillsbury looked most disappointed.

"I'm afraid so."

Pillsbury put down his clipboard. "Then it could have been anything really, any poison. Anyway, ladies, I am afraid I can't let you take a sample of Mrs Jones's hair, not after her daughter and granddaughter specifically asked me not to."

Maude sidled up to him and gave him what she no doubt imagined was a seductive smile. "But they're not benefactors of the will and my sisters and I are," she said. "Doesn't that count for anything?"

Pillsbury looked discomfited. "I'm afraid not. It would only be of use if the will said you could take some of her hair, but obviously it didn't, so I have to abide by the wishes of the next of kin."

"Quite right," Aunt Agnes said. "Well Maude, you stay here and have a little chat with Pillsbury and we'll wait for you in the car."

Maude made to follow us, but Agnes clamped a hand on the shoulder. "We don't mind. There is no need to protest. We will wait in the car."

It took a few moments for Agnes's wishes to

dawn on Maude. "Oh, I see," she said, nodding slowly as she spoke.

When Pillsbury wasn't looking, Aunt Agnes made a kissing motion with her lips. Maude looked puzzled. Agnes took me by the arm and ushered me outside. "Okay, I'm hoping Maude gets the hint to keep Pillsbury occupied and then you can go in and cut some of Euphemia's hair."

"Why me?" I protested. "Why can't you do it?"

"Because you're younger and more agile than we are," Aunt Agnes said with a smile. She handed me a small pair of scissors. "Don't be too fussy about it. Just cut some off."

"What if Pillsbury sees me?" I said.

"Valkyrie, it is imperative that you get some of that hair, whether he sees you or not. Get the hair first and worry about him seeing you later. If the worst comes to the worst, use your vampire speed."

I rolled my eyes. "This really isn't fair."

Aunt Agnes waved her hand at me and gave me a gentle shove. The front door was still open a little. I poked my head around and peeped inside. Aunt Maude had Pillsbury in a passionate embrace, but she had one eye fixed on the door. I gave her a little wave. With her one hand behind Pillsbury's neck, she waved me into the next room.

I dropped to the ground and crawled as fast as I could into the other room. I thought the door opening might alert Pillsbury, but he didn't seem to notice.

Once inside the room, I stood up. It was a plain white room with stainless steel drawers, no doubt filled with bodies, just like on TV shows. I crossed to the nearest one and opened it. There, to my horror, was Euphemia Jones. I don't know what I had expected. She looked pretty good for a dead person. I grabbed the scissors and cut off a huge chunk of her hair and popped it in the plastic bag Aunt Agnes had given me. I shoved the bag in my pocket and pushed the drawer shut.

"Is somebody in there?" I heard Pillsbury say.

"I didn't hear anything," Maude said.

I looked around for a hiding place and noticed a door at the back of the room. I don't know why I hadn't noticed it before. I ran over to it. It was locked from the inside, so I quickly flipped the lock and let myself out.

I at once tripped over a rubbish bin at the back door. It fell to the ground with a loud clatter. Okay, it was time to use my vampire speed. I hightailed it out of there. When I reached the road, I resumed my normal pace and walked over to Aunt Agnes's car. "Here you are," I said handing Agnes the bag.

"My goodness gracious me, Valkyrie, did you leave her any hair at all?"

"You said not to be too fussy about it," I said.

Aunt Agnes chuckled. "I've already filled out the forms. Let's go to the post office now."

"What about Maude?" I asked.

"Oh, I forgot all about her," Agnes said. "Dorothy, why don't you go and get her?"

Dorothy did as she asked. "So, that will tell us if it was arsenic or one of several heavy metals," I said to Aunt Agnes, "but how we are going to track it down if it's another type of poison?"

"I've been thinking about that," Agnes said. "Jezabeth is a wealthy woman. She could have easily stayed in a motel. I thought she was only staying in one of our cottages to bother us because that's the type of thing she would do, but maybe she wanted to stay in the cottage so she could remove any evidence of poison in her mother's cottage."

I thought it over. "That doesn't add up, because she said she couldn't stay in her mother's cottage. If she was the murderer, then she would have made some excuse and asked to stay in her mother's cottage. Then she would have had all the time in the world to hide the evidence."

It was Aunt Agnes's turn to disagree. "No, I don't think so, because at that point the police hadn't ruled it natural causes and the cottage was out of bounds."

"I suppose you're right," I said. "Who do you think it was, Aunt Agnes?"

"It's obviously someone we're overlooking," she said.

CHAPTER 13

"I don't think we should take in any new boarders until this whole matter of Gorgona's murder is solved," Aunt Agnes said. "It makes me nervous, what with Lucas away and everything."

The mention of Lucas made me sad. I had been missing him dreadfully. "We don't have any bookings for a while, anyway. I'll put a notice on the website saying we're full for the next two weeks."

Aunt Agnes nodded her approval. "That's a good idea."

I couldn't get to sleep, and I was certain that it didn't have anything to do with the coffee I'd had late that afternoon. I had an uneasy feeling something was going to happen. I had sometimes felt that way in the past and nothing had happened, but that was no consolation.

I tossed and turned, and then wasn't sure whether I had drifted off to sleep briefly, or whether I had been awake the whole time. I was groggy and uncomfortable.

I debated getting up and making myself a cup of tea and a Vegemite sandwich but decided against it. Sometime later, I looked at the phone beside my bed. It was 1.30 in the morning. I was missing Lucas, and the uneasy feeling hadn't gone away. If only I was able to be in contact with him, but it was too dangerous. We couldn't take any chances that The Other would track down my parents.

With the realisation I wouldn't be able to sleep, I staggered out of bed. I didn't put on my lights, because I figured it would be just my luck that one of the aunts would see my lights, think something was wrong, and come over, and then I'd never get any sleep.

I looked through my herbal teas—I wasn't going to risk the caffeine in normal tea—and decided upon a lemon and ginger tea. I dropped the tea bag in my coffee mug and boiled the electric care jug. Now that I was up, I wasn't really hungry. I wondered whether I should make some Vegemite toast or maybe eat some chocolate chip biscuits. Maybe both.

I was thinking it over when I thought I heard rain falling lightly. I walked to the front door to look out. It was then I noticed movement over by the *Game of Thrones* cottage. Maybe, it was a kangaroo. I was shutting the door when I saw a light flicker inside the cottage. Well, that certainly wasn't a kangaroo.

I ran back inside and grabbed my phone and called Aunt Agnes. It rang out. I called Maude next, but it went straight to voicemail. The same happened when I called Dorothy. Surely, they hadn't turned off their phones in the night? I debated what to do.

If I ran to the manor, the intruder would likely see me because mine was the furthest cottage from the manor. I figured I could skirt behind the other cottages. Still, this was an opportunity to catch the murderer. I had vampire speed and, hopefully, the murderer wasn't involved with The Other. I was of the opinion the murderer was a blackmail victim of Euphemia and Ethelbert's. And I figured the murderer was at the cottage to destroy evidence.

With a sudden burst of bravery, I ran to my front gate. Once through it, I ran towards the beach with vampire speed, skirted around behind a clump of banksias trees, and came up behind the *Game of Thrones* cottage.

I could see a light flickering inside. I was in bare feet, so I moved more carefully this time. It wasn't sand here and some of the undergrowth was quite prickly. I moved as quietly as I could. When I was just outside the cottage gate, which thankfully was open, something dug into the tender part of the ball of my foot. The pain made me cry out, so I clamped my hand firmly over my mouth.

I rubbed the underneath of my foot before creeping up to the window and looking inside.

To my utter surprise, there was a tea light candle flickering away on the kitchen table. As I tried to process what that could mean, something heavy hit me over the back of the head.

Everything went black.

When I awoke, I saw a dragon on the ceiling. I was surrounded by fire. "I must be in King's Landing," I said aloud in my confusion.

It took me a while to realise what had happened. I was in the *Game of Thrones* cottage and it actually was on fire. My head hurt and my lungs ached. I crawled towards the front door, just as it opened, and Aunt Agnes and Aunt Maude pulled me outside. Aunt Dorothy was already hosing down the building.

They pulled me outside the front gate and sat me down on the grass. "What happened?" Aunt Agnes asked me.

I gulped fresh air before answering. "I saw a light in the cottage so I called you all, but you didn't answer so I decided to investigate. Someone hit me from behind."

"Did you see who it was?" Aunt Agnes asked me.

I shook my head. "Ouch, my head hurts!"

"We've called for fire and ambulance," she said.

"I'm fine," I said, but Aunt Agnes had already left to hose the building with a garden hose. I wanted to help, but I figured there were only three garden hoses.

Breena appeared in her human form. "Fire, bad," she said.

I felt sick to my stomach. "Yes," was all I could manage to say.

The aunts put the fire out just as the fire engine arrived, followed soon after by the ambulance. I didn't hear what the fire fighters said to the aunts, but they all went inside the cottage while a paramedic shone a torch in my eyes.

"How long were you unconscious for?" she asked me.

"Um, but how would I know?" I asked. "I suppose it wasn't long because I figure whoever hit me over the head started the fire, and the aunts seem to have arrived pretty much soon after."

"We'd better take you to hospital for observation. You likely have concussion."

"No, I'll be all right," I said. She tried to talk me into going with them, but I flatly refused. The two paramedics went over and spoke with Aunt Agnes and gestured to me throughout. I certainly hoped she didn't try to make me go with them, but to my relief, she didn't.

After the fire fighters and paramedics left, Aunt Agnes and Aunt Maude helped me into the house. Aunt Agnes insisted I lie on the antique Victorian chaise in the living room. "You'll have to stay here all night," she said. "One of us will sit up with you just in case you do have concussion. Still, the witches' brew will put you to rights."

"How bad is the cottage?" I asked her.

"It hasn't been affected structurally, but it's pretty bad inside. Maude is in the kitchen calling the insurance company right now."

"Did you see who it was?" Breena asked me.

I looked at her in shock. It was the most she had ever said.

"No, I didn't see anything," I said, "but they must have seen me."

"Obviously, because they hit you," Dorothy said. "If they didn't see you, they wouldn't have hit you."

I clutched my head with both hands. "I didn't mean that. I meant, they must've seen me sneaking around."

Aunt Agnes handed me a goblet of witches' brew. "Drink up!"

I took a large gulp of witches' brew and then said, "I saw a light inside the cottage. I saw someone outside the cottage and I thought it was a kangaroo or something, but then I saw a light moving around inside the cottage, so I went over. When I got there, I saw somebody had put a tea light candle on the kitchen table."

"Why would they have done that?" Dorothy asked me.

"I expect so I would sneak up and look through a window, just like I did," I said. "Obviously, they were behind me all the time."

"You don't think it was the tea light candle that you saw from the old cottage?" Agnes asked me.

I shook my head and then said, "Ouch." I would have to stop moving my head. "No, I could see the light moving through the cottage. And you know what! I used my vampire speed to come up behind the cottage and I only stopped when I reached the cottage."

"Interesting." Aunt Agnes tapped her chin. "Well then, there must've been some evidence in the cottage, because whoever was there was trying to destroy it."

"We should go and have another look," I said.

"We'll do it in broad daylight," Aunt Agnes said, "in the morning. I doubt the intruder will be back tonight. And maybe they have destroyed the evidence already."

"I hope not," I said. "They wouldn't have had much time, because I was at the cottage moments after I saw them going inside the cottage."

"We can only hope."

Aunt Maude walked into the room. "Agnes, they're sending an insurance assessor."

"Did they say when?"

Maude shrugged. "They're calling us tomorrow."

The doorbell reverberated through the house.

"The police," Aunt Agnes said. "They took their sweet time."

She presently showed in Detective Oakes and Detective Mason.

"So, did the paramedics verify that you received a blow to the head?" Oakes asked me.

I glared at him. "Yes. There's a huge lump there, and the skin is broken."

Detective Mason yawned and rubbed his eyes.

"Would you like some coffee?" Aunt Agnes asked him.

"That would be great, thanks," Oakes said. Mason simply nodded.

"So tell me what happened," he added.

"I couldn't sleep, so I got up to make a cup of tea, and I thought it was raining. I stuck my head out the door to check, and I saw someone go to the cottage."

"And what did you do then?" Oakes asked me.

"I ran back inside and called each one of my aunts in turn, but they didn't answer, so I decided I should sneak around and peek from a distance."

Oakes's eyebrows shot skyward. "What? It didn't occur to you that such actions could be dangerous?"

I felt too weak and sick to be lectured. "If I had

tried to run to the manor, the intruder would have seen me. I wasn't going to confront them, of course, but I thought I could snoop."

Mason made a tut-tutting sound, while Oakes waved one hand at me. "Go on." He looked back at Mason. "Are you writing this down?"

Mason pulled a notepad and pen from his pocket. "Yes."

"I had seen a light flickering around inside the cottage and it was still flickering by the time I reached the cottage. When I looked through the window, the only light I could see was a tea light candle sitting on the kitchen table. That's when someone hit me over the back of the head. That's all I remember until I woke up inside the cottage and the aunts pulled me outside."

"Are you certain you were hit over the head *outside* the cottage?" Oakes asked me.

"Yes, I'm absolutely positive," I said. "I was outside looking through the window, wondering why there was a tea light candle alight on the table."

"So, somebody dragged you inside when you were unconscious and set fire to the cottage."

"Yes, Oakes. Obviously, it's a case of attempted murder," Detective Mason said.

Aunt Agnes returned and handed them each a steaming mug of coffee. "Are you now going to consider that Euphemia Jones was murdered, after all?"

Oakes looked most uncomfortable. "The two incidents might not be related."

"Euphemia Jones was renting the *Game of Thrones* cottage, and tonight there was an intruder in the cottage. They clearly lured my niece to look through the window by placing a tea light candle on the table to make her think there was an intruder inside the cottage, and then they attacked her, dragged her into the cottage, and set fire to the cottage. Why would they have done that if they didn't want to do away with my niece and most likely do away with any evidence of poison?"

Oakes rubbed his chin. "We will be in touch over this matter. Ms Jasper, I suggest you stay with your boyfriend for the present. Where is he?"

"He's visiting relatives in Sydney," I said. I hoped Oakes wasn't working for The Other because now he knew for sure that Lucas wasn't in town.

Oakes nodded slowly. "Shouldn't you be in hospital?"

"Yes, she should, but she refused to go," Aunt

Agnes said. "The youth of today! Still, one of us will sit up with her all night to make sure she's all right."

"And where was your niece from France when all this was happening?" Detective Oakes asked Aunt Agnes.

"She and I were sitting together in the kitchen drinking cocoa," Aunt Agnes said.

Oakes narrowed his eyes. "Wasn't that a rather strange hour to be awake?"

"We had been watching reruns of *The X-Files* and we were both too scared to sleep," Aunt Agnes said. "I'd forgotten how scary some of those episodes were."

"And between what hours were you having cocoa?" Mason's pen hovered over his notepad.

"We started watching *The X-Files* just after eight. We watched several episodes in a row and then we both said we were too scared to sleep, and so we made cocoa," Aunt Agnes said. "My phone had switched itself to silent and when I finally looked down, I saw that Valkyrie had called. She didn't answer when I called back. That's why I went outside and saw the cottage on fire."

"So, your niece was with you the whole time."

Aunt Agnes nodded. "Oh yes. She was never out of my sight."

Detective Oakes had barely sipped his coffee, whereas Mason was slurping his greedily in between speaking. "Ms Jasper," Oakes said, "it's probably best if you don't go back to your cottage at this point. Stay in the manor with your aunts until we can get to the bottom of this matter." He turned to Aunt Agnes. "Have you been in touch with your insurance company yet?"

Aunt Agnes nodded. "They're sending an investigator."

Oakes waved his finger at me. "That was a very foolish thing that you did, Ms Jasper. Try to resist such impulsive urges in the future." He turned to leave but then stopped and turned back to me. "You said you saw a figure. Could you see if it was a man or a woman, or whether they were tall or short?"

"No, it was too far away."

He nodded. "That will be all for now, but we might have to question you again. Well, good night, ladies." He pulled out a card and handed it to Aunt Agnes. "Call me if anything else happens."

With that, Aunt Maude showed the detectives to the door.

"I don't like this. I don't like this at all," Aunt

Agnes said. "I find it strange that someone would try to murder you, Valkyrie."

"But somebody did murder Gorgona," Dorothy pointed out.

Aunt Agnes shook her head vigorously. "They murdered *Gorgona*, sure. We know Ethelbert was murdered because he blackmailed Mrs Mumbles and Killian Cosgrove. We don't know why Gorgona was murdered, but if she was murdered because she was blackmailing people, then why would her murderer try to murder Valkyrie?"

I was trying to make sense of it all. I drank the rest of my witches' brew and Aunt Agnes immediately filled up my goblet. "That will help heal any concussion you have," she said. "But you'll have to take it easy all day tomorrow."

I pulled a face.

"Then what are you thinking, Agnes?" Maude asked her.

"I'm thinking that somebody seems to have a particular grudge against Valkyrie, and I find that strange. I can't see how that relates to Gorgona's murder. After the intruder hit Valkyrie over the back of the head, they could easily have left, but no, they dragged her into the cottage and set fire to it. Something is wrong, very wrong."

CHAPTER 14

$\mathcal{U}$pon awakening, I looked around the room, disoriented, wondering where I was. It took me a moment or two to realise I was in the living room of Mugwort Manor and not in my own cottage. The events of the previous night flooded back to me.

Now that the witches' brew had healed me, I could think more clearly. Sure, I could understand it if someone had knocked me over the back of the head in an attempt to get away, but this had been a deliberate setup. Someone had put the candle on the dining room table to entice me into the cottage. No doubt, they only did that when they saw me heading their way. The whole thing couldn't have been premeditated, because I woke up on my own accord and only happened to see someone at the *Game of Thrones* cottage. Still, however, somebody had tried to murder me.

But that didn't make any sense. Who would have a grudge against me and how was that connected with Gorgona? All right, we were related and we were both vampires, but I didn't stand to inherit anything in her will, so it's not as if a beneficiary had wanted me out of the way for financial gain.

I got off the chaise and walked to the kitchen, the delightful aroma of coffee beckoning me.

Aunt Maude looked up, surprised. "Valkyrie! You were out like a light when Cary and I checked on you only a few minutes ago."

I headed straight for the coffee machine and dropped in a pod. It wasn't until I was sitting down at the kitchen table with some caffeine in me that I spoke. "I was trying to figure out who would have wanted to kill me."

All three aunts nodded. "We were trying to figure that out too," Aunt Agnes said. "Obviously, the perpetrator saw you heading for the cottage."

"But I did so at vampire speed," I pointed out.

"How far out of your cottage were you when

you took off at vampire speed?" Aunt Agnes asked me.

I thought back. "I snuck out the front door and out the front gate. Yes, it was only when I was out the front gate that I took off at vampire speed."

"Then that's no help at all," Agnes said.

Aunt Maude looked up in surprise. "How so, Agnes?"

"I was thinking that if Valkyrie had come out of her cottage at vampire speed and continued that way until she got to the *Game of Thrones* cottage, then whoever was in Euphemia's cottage must have been a vampire, because a normal person would have been unable to see her."

Dorothy nodded slowly. "Yes, that occurred to me too."

"So we're none the wiser," I lamented, reaching over to pat Cary.

The aunts nodded. "After breakfast, we will go over and have a look around," Agnes said. "We can't look as though we've been there, though, or the insurance investigator won't like it."

I agreed. "With any luck, whoever it was didn't make off with all the evidence. Like I said last night, they couldn't have been there long."

Aunt Agnes nodded slowly. "You know, the more I think about it, the more I think it was a vampire," she said. "You said there wasn't much time between the time you saw the intruder outside the cottage, and the time you actually went to the cottage. Still, the intruder had time to see you, plan their attack, and light a candle. I'm thinking someone probably had to have vampire speed to do that."

Aunt Dorothy waved one hand in the air for silence, dropping her piece of toast on the table as she did so. She grunted in disgust and put it back on her plate.

Aunt Maude turned to her. "Oh, there's peanut butter and Vegemite on the table."

"Calm your farm, Maude," Dorothy said. "I'll clean it up."

Maude rolled her eyes. "How anyone can put peanut butter and Vegemite on the same piece of toast is beyond me."

"Now I forgot what I was going to say, and it was important," Dorothy said.

"It couldn't have been too important if you forgot it," Maude countered.

Aunt Dorothy folded her arms over her chest. "It really annoys me when people say things like that. People can forget important things just as easily as they can forget non-important things."

"Did you remember what you were going to say?" I asked Dorothy to stop the bickering.

Dorothy looked up at the ceiling for a moment before answering. "Yes, thank goodness, I do, as a matter of fact. All our assumptions about timing are based on the fact that you saw the shadowy figure outside the cottage. But what if the intruder had already spent some time at the cottage and you saw them leaving rather than going to the cottage?"

"I don't understand," I said, thoroughly confused.

"I mean, what if the intruder had been there for some time and then you saw them leaving. They saw you watching them and then decided to set a trap for you."

"I doubt they would have seen me," I said. "It was dark."

"But you saw them, didn't you!" Dorothy said.

I nodded slowly. "Yes, you do have a point."

I noticed Aunt Agnes and Aunt Maude exchanging glances and I could see they didn't agree with Dorothy.

"We might know more when we have a look

around," I said in the hope of pre-empting a fresh round of bickering.

We all finished our breakfast hurriedly and walked over to the cottage. "Don't ruin any evidence," Aunt Agnes cautioned. "Valkyrie, show us the very point you emerged from the bushes."

I led them over to the spot. "It was dark, but I was pretty sure it was here."

"Make doubly sure," Aunt Agnes said. "If we know where you were, then we will have a better idea where the intruder could have been, and maybe they left some evidence around. Otherwise, it's too wide an area to pinpoint anything."

I pointed to some wattle bushes. "I'm pretty sure I came out there, and I walked over to the cottage directly ahead. I had bare feet. I remember something stuck into the ball of my foot hard and hurt my foot."

"There are no stones around here," Maude said.

Aunt Agnes agreed. "Find out what you stepped on, because it might have been something the intruder dropped."

"Okay, well, I came out here as far as I can tell, and I headed straight for the gate which was open," I said, motioning with my arm. It was hen I noticed the little stones. "That's when I stepped on those pebbles." I pointed.

Aunt Agnes walked past me and picked one up. "This is not a pebble."

"What is it?" I asked.

The aunts all looked at each other and shrugged.

"Look, there are a few more," I said, pointing to several of the pretty pebbles or whatever they were.

Aunt Agnes bent down and picked them up. "This might be nothing, but it could be important," she said, pocketing them all. "Let's look through the cottage."

"Hang on a moment. I'll take a photo of one," I said.

Aunt Agnes held out her hand, palm upwards, with the pebbles in it. "Why do you want to take a photo, Valkyrie? We have several pebbles. It's not as if we'll lose them."

"I'm going to do a reverse image search on the Internet," I told her. "Just hold one in your palm so I can get a decent photo of it."

She did as I asked, and I took a close-up photo on my phone. The others went into the cottage. Aunt Agnes looked over her shoulder at me. "Valkyrie, go back to the manor now and rest."

I held up my hand. "Just give me a moment. I've gotta find out what these things are."

She disappeared into the cottage. I thought I would have trouble with the reverse image search, but I got an instant hit.

A castor bean.

I shrugged and walked back to the manor.

"Did you find out what it was?" Aunt Agnes asked me when she arrived back from the cottage.

"Yes, it's just a castor bean," I told her.

Maude and Agnes gasped, while Dorothy said, "Maybe, Gorgona had constipation. That's why she was always so cranky."

"No!" Aunt Agnes exclaimed. "The most deadly poison in the world is ricin. It's made from castor beans."

"But we found actual whole castor beans, not ricin," I said. "Wouldn't ricin have to be made in a lab or something?"

When the aunts shot me blank looks, I said, "Don't worry, I'll google it."

Once more, it didn't take me long to find the information. "You'll never believe this!" I said. "Like Aunt Agnes said, ricin is a deadly poison, and there are instructions for making it online."

"So, someone simply had to find and copy the instructions online?" Agnes asked me.

I shook my head. "No, there's also an article by an academic that says the online instructions are inaccurate."

Aunt Agnes opened her mouth, but I pushed on. "But he says that the beans themselves are deadly if someone chews them and eats them."

Aunt Agnes held out the beans in her hand and poked them with one finger. "But why would anyone chew one up and eat it?" she asked. "Are you sure they have to be chewed, Valkyrie? Maybe we should go back and search the cottage more thoroughly."

I shook my head. "No, the beans have to be split open, and that's what I'm trying to say."

We all traipsed back to the cottage at Aunt Agnes's urging. "What are we looking for exactly?" Maude asked.

I looked past her at the coffee machine. "There! Her drip filter coffee!" I said, and then I pointed to the coffee grinder next to it. "Gorgona loved her coffee!"

We all hurried over to the grinder. Aunt Agnes took a piece of baking paper and spread it over the kitchen table. "Is everyone still wearing their gloves?"

We all nodded. "Is it safe to breathe it in?" Aunt Maude asked. "Maybe I should take Cary outside." Without waiting for a response, she opened the front door and stood just outside, clutching Cary to her.

"There are castor beans in her coffee grinder!" I exclaimed. "Look at them! But wouldn't it make her coffee taste weird? Surely, she would have noticed something amiss with her coffee."

Aunt Agnes pushed some of the beans around with a gloved finger. "It looks as though there are more castor beans than coffee beans in here."

Aunt Dorothy picked up a large bottle of syrup. "Remember, Gorgona had a sweet tooth? She must have put a lot of this caramel syrup into her coffee. This would have disguised the flavour of anything, even the coffee."

"Then do we tell the police?" I asked Aunt Agnes.

She tapped her head. "I'm wondering how we can tell them that we discovered this without admitting we were snooping."

"Maybe I should call the police and say I stepped on something and put it in my pocket in case it was important. I could say I forgot about it until this morning when I pulled it out of my pocket and then did a reverse Google search and found it was a castor bean." I said that all in one breath.

Aunt Agnes shrugged. "Why not! The detectives can take it or leave it. If they do, they will realise Gorgona's death was not an accident. Let's give it a great deal of thought first, though. We had better be certain we've covered our tracks. And now we have to get ready for the funeral."

I tapped myself on the side of the head. "The funeral! I'd forgotten all about it."

CHAPTER 15

*W*e arrived at the cemetery for the funeral. The place seemed deserted. "I wonder where the graveside is?" Aunt Maude said.

"I'll pop into the office and ask," Aunt Agnes said. Thankfully, she had parked directly outside the office.

"Follow me," she said when she came out moments later.

We walked up a rise, and at the top, I could see the funeral director consultant, who at once hurried up the short hill to greet us. "I'm so sorry for your loss," she said, tottering on her heels. "I'll keep out of your way, but should you need anything, just wave to me. I'm here to help, but I won't get in your way. This is *your* funeral."

"To the contrary, it's Euphemia Jones's funeral," Dorothy said in an angry tone.

Agnes took her by the arm and guided her down the hill to the gravesite. Jezabeth and Hemlock were already there, standing beside a coffin raised on a mechanical structure quite high off the ground. We walked up to them. Jezabeth didn't acknowledge us, but Hemlock walked over and thrust a piece of paper into Aunt Agnes's hands.

"What's this?" Aunt Agnes said.

"It's an invoice for the flowers and the fireworks," Hemlock said. "You need to reimburse me, Agnes."

Aunt Agnes arched one eyebrow. "You expect me to pay for this?"

"Of course not!" Hemlock snapped. "Grannie can pay for it. Didn't you get money out of her account to pay for the funeral?"

Aunt Agnes crossed her arms over her chest. "I can't pay for this, Hemlock. Legally, I can only pay the funeral directors' bill and the cemetery bill."

Hemlock narrowed her eyes. "Well, someone's gotta pay for it!"

"It seems you already have," Aunt Maude said.

Hemlock pouted. "You don't need to make a big deal out of this and cause all this trouble at Grannie's funeral. We need to give Grannie a good send-off. She was a vampire, after all." She said the latter in hushed tones and looked around herself as she spoke.

"Well then, it was you and your mother who decided what to have for the service, or lack thereof," Aunt Agnes said.

Hemlock stormed off. She ran over and clutched her mother's arm. Jezabeth spoke with Hemlock and then walked over to us.

"Why aren't you paying for the flowers and the fireworks?" she asked through tight lips.

Aunt Agnes sighed. "Jezabeth, I've already explained to your daughter that the estate can only pay for the funeral director's costs and the cemetery costs. You have to pay for anything else. You know, you could have arranged for the funeral director to bill you for some flowers, and then the estate could have paid for them."

I stared at the flowers. They seemed familiar. I wondered if they had been picked from the gardens at Mugwort Manor. "Can I see that invoice?" I asked Aunt Agnes.

I had suspected something was amiss, and I was right. The receipt was from a florist, all right, but it appeared to have been for fifteen dollars, and a zero had been added in a different coloured pen. Also, the word 'fireworks' was written underneath in different handwriting. I looked up at Hemlock. "I didn't know florists sold fireworks."

"You're a troublemaker!" she yelled at me. She said some more words which I could not repeat.

"Hush, Hemlock," her mother said. "Behave yourself for once."

Hemlock narrowed her eyes and for a minute I thought there would be a terrible scene, but Jezabeth walked back towards the coffin.

"I'm going to say a few words," Jezabeth said, "and then anyone else can feel free to speak after I do. My mother was an unpleasant woman. Still, she had her good points. I hadn't seen her in decades, but I'm sorry she's gone. If there hadn't been all these false accusations that she was murdered, then I would have been able to grieve her properly. Unfortunately, all these allegations about murder have stopped me from being able to grieve my own mother." After she finished speaking, she shot Agnes a vicious look.

Aunt Agnes stepped forward. She spoke

eloquently about Gorgona, and while she didn't exactly say anything nice about her, she didn't say anything horrid, either. I was surprised she was able to speak for so long without saying anything at all, really.

"Would you like to say something now?" Jezabeth asked Hemlock.

"Yes, I'm going to do an interpretive dance," she said, "and then I will let off the fireworks."

"Fireworks are thoroughly illegal," Aunt Maude told her. "You won't be allowed to light any fireworks. You should know that."

Hemlock merely shot her a nasty look. She had a little amplifier that she plugged into her iPhone. I hadn't seen one like it before. She turned it on and turned up the volume. To me, the music sounded something like the Arabian nights with overtones of death metal music.

Hemlock at once went into what she had called an interpretive dance, but to me looked more like a drunken belly dance gone wrong. She swung this way and that way, moving her hands out to the sides like a venomous snake striking, and then swinging her hands back again. I hadn't realised she had gymnastic abilities, and if she hadn't been heavily under the influence of illegal substances, the dance might have looked quite good. It was only when she began to take off her clothes that I became alarmed.

"Is she taking off her clothes?" Aunt Dorothy asked, leaning forward to get a better look.

Aunt Agnes adjusted her glasses and then gave up and looked over the top of them. "I do believe she is. Oh my goodness, that tattoo must have been painful. I didn't know you could get them there."

I wasn't sure whether to laugh or cry. I stood there, unable to look away from Hemlock doing an interpretive dance a.k.a. a strip.

I noticed the funeral consultant standing in the background, her mouth hanging open in shock. After a while, she hurried over to Jezabeth and whispered in her ear. Jezabeth must not have said anything to her liking, because she in turn hurried over to Agnes. "It's illegal to take one's clothes off in public," she said, clearly horrified.

"I'm afraid I have no control over Hemlock," Agnes said. "Perhaps you should speak to her mother again."

The poor woman merely hurried away.

Hemlock stopped gyrating and said, "And now for the next performance."

Aunt Agnes said, "I think you had better put

your clothes back on in a hurry, Hemlock. I think the funeral consultant lady might be calling the police."

"Not the cops again!" Hemlock said, making me wonder what she meant. At any rate, she did put her clothes back on. We all breathed a sigh of relief.

"And now for the next part," Hemlock proclaimed loudly. "We have to give Grannie a proper send off. I liked Grannie. It was a pity she had to die." She pulled something out of her handbag. She lit it and threw it into the empty grave.

"Oh no," said Aunt Agnes.

"Maybe we should leave now?" Aunt Dorothy said hopefully.

I stepped forward. "I vote with Aunt Dorothy!"

"Why didn't it go off?" Hemlock yelled in a rage. She pulled more fireworks from her handbag. She lit them all and threw them into the grave.

All of a sudden, there was a mighty explosion. Pretty colours of green, red, and yellow burst forth from the grave. An explosion shook the ground and the coffin flew into the air.

It all seemed to happen in slow motion. The lid flew off when the coffin landed in a tree.

Gorgona's body toppled out and fell directly into the grave.

"Grannie!" Hemlock yelled and jumped in after her.

Jezabeth rounded on the aunts. "Do something!" she yelled. "This has turned into a disaster! It's a farce!"

"She's *your* daughter," Aunt Agnes said. I could see she was doing her best not to laugh.

"This is all your fault!" Jezabeth screamed.

"How do you figure that?" Aunt Agnes asked her.

"You wouldn't give Hemlock the money for the roses or the fireworks and you upset her."

The logic of that escaped me, but the logic of just about everything Jezabeth and Hemlock did escaped me. Aunt Agnes walked over to the grave and reached in for Hemlock. As her face appeared over the top, I saw that her eyebrows were singed off and her face was bright red.

Just as Aunt Agnes was about to haul Hemlock over the edge, Hemlock said, "You're such a troublemaker, Aunt Agnes."

Aunt Agnes released her hands. Hemlock fell back into the grave.

It was all too much for the funeral consultant. She sprinted to her car and drove away at speed.

"Can we leave now?" I said.

"Yes," Aunt Agnes said.

The four of us hurried off in the other direction, leaving Hemlock and Jezabeth to scream obscenities behind us.

CHAPTER 16

"I'll be pleased when Jezabeth and Hemlock leave town," Aunt Agnes said as she sped away from the cemetery.

"How will they get the coffin out of the tree?"

Aunt Agnes swerved to avoid a rabbit that ran out in front of the car. "Not our problem, Valkyrie."

"When were you going to speak to Joyce Batson, Agnes?" Aunt Dorothy piped up from the back seat.

Aunt Agnes sighed. "I suppose I should go and see her now."

"We'll go with you," Maude offered.

Aunt Agnes shook her head. "I'll take you and Dorothy home to keep an eye on Breena. If the police come back, we can't have them questioning

187

her. Keep her out of sight at all times—lock her in the secret room if you have to."

"Is it safe, though?" asked Maude.

Aunt Agnes quickly glanced across at her. "What do you mean?"

"I mean she can get into the tunnel from the secret room."

"Breena has been in the tunnel before," I said. "And if you're wondering if she's working for The Other, remember that she didn't tell anyone where my parents were."

"That's true, but…" Aunt Maude's voice trailed away.

"Maude, do you think Breena had something to do with Gorgona's death?" Aunt Agnes asked her.

Maude shrugged. "I have no idea, to be honest. Still, we can't discount it as a possibility. Not while we don't have a clue who did it, at any rate."

"We do have a few suspects," I said.

"And I'm on my way to speak to one of those suspects now," Agnes said. "And if Joyce didn't do it, hopefully she might offer some insight into the situation."

No one spoke again until Agnes dropped Maude and Dorothy back at the manor. "Call me immediately if something happens," she said to them. "Don't hesitate."

When Aunt Agnes parked the car outside the antique shop, I said, "You must be a bit upset about Joyce being a suspect. She's a good friend of yours, isn't she?"

"I've known her for years," Aunt Agnes said. "I'd be surprised if she did murder Gorgona. Very surprised." She straightened up and picked up her handbag. "Still, people have surprised me in the past."

Joyce's face lit up when she saw Agnes, no doubt as Agnes was one of her best customers. "Oh, Agnes, great to see you. I have several items from a deceased estate coming in next week."

"Actually, I came here to speak with you about a deceased estate," Agnes said.

I gave myself a mental slap on the side of the head. I had completely forgotten that the aunts were inheriting some of Gorgona's antique furniture.

Joyce's mouth formed a perfect O. "You are?"

Agnes nodded slowly. "My sisters and I are the executors of an estate for one of the boarders, who happened to be my cousin, Euphemia Jones."

Joyce looked thoroughly shocked. "That awful

woman was your cousin? Oh, I'm terribly sorry, Agnes, I didn't mean to insult you."

Aunt Agnes waved one hand at her. "Think nothing of it."

"So, your cousin was married to the man who was murdered!"

Agnes nodded. "Yes, that's right, but we didn't actually know she was our cousin. We hadn't seen her in many years, and she had legally changed her name."

Joyce continued to look shocked. She was leaning back against a marble topped, burr walnut credenza, clutching the marble top with both hands. "Why, that's amazing!" she said. "And you say you're the executor of her will?"

"Yes, along with Dorothy and Maude," Agnes said. "Euphemia's daughter and granddaughter inherit a lot more than we do. I expect she didn't trust them to be executors, and I'm surprised she left us anything, truth be told. Anyway, as far as the antiques are concerned, my sisters and I get fifty percent of them and Euphemia's daughter gets the other fifty percent. When the antiques are sorted out, we won't be able to keep all of them."

"Did she have many?" Joyce asked.

Aunt Agnes nodded. "She had a huge house, and it's absolutely jam-packed full of antiques."

Joyce appeared to be recovering from the shock. "Do you know which antiques you're getting?"

Aunt Agnes chuckled. "I assume it won't be the good ones. Still, if Euphemia's daughter thinks we want any antiques in particular, then those will be the ones she wants. I should pretend we want all the poor quality ones."

Joyce did not chuckle along with Agnes. "She doesn't sound like a nice person."

Aunt Agnes pulled a face. "She isn't. Anyway, Joyce, when the antiques situation is sorted out, and Dorothy, Maude, and I decide which ones we would like to keep, then I'll call you to give us prices on the rest of them."

"You know I'll do right by you," Joyce said. "I'll give you good prices."

Aunt Agnes nodded solemnly. "I know you will, Joyce. Now, we have to speak about a delicate matter." She looked around the shop. "Since you don't have any customers, I suppose I can bring it up now."

I noticed Joyce's face was white and drawn. "What is it, Agnes?" she said.

Aunt Agnes leant forward and spoke in a

conspiratorial tone. "We think Euphemia Jones was murdered."

"Murdered!" Joyce shrieked and then stuck her hand over her mouth.

To me, she seemed genuinely surprised. Or maybe she was just a good actor.

"Do the police know who did it?"

Aunt Agnes shook her head. "No, they don't have a clue. At first, they thought it was natural causes until Valkyrie was hit over the back of the head last night when disturbing an intruder to Euphemia's cottage."

Joyce turned her attention to me. "Are you all right?"

She didn't seem to have any malice towards me, but if she was working for The Other, then it wouldn't be personal. It occurred to me that she had been here in town for years, keeping friends with Agnes. What's more, the matter of antiques would give her entry into Mugwort Manor. "I'm all right now," I said. "It was a pretty nasty experience."

"Did you see who did it?" Joyce asked me. "Did you catch a glimpse of the person?"

"No, I didn't," I said. "It was too dark. I only

saw them from a distance and then I went over to the cottage. That's when they took me by surprise."

"A dreadful business," Joyce muttered. "A dreadful business indeed."

"And now to the delicate matter," Aunt Agnes said. "At first, the police didn't realise Euphemia was murdered. On the other hand, my sisters and I did know it was murder, so we had already started investigating."

Joyce's eyes grew wide. "You had?"

Agnes nodded and pushed on. "Because we are executors of Euphemia's will, we were able to look through all her paperwork, and we found evidence she had been blackmailing people. Of course, we knew her husband had been blackmailing people and that's why Killian Cosgrove murdered him, but I'm afraid to say we also found something incriminating about you, Joyce."

Joyce's hand flew to her throat. "Me?" she squeaked.

"Yes, we found that you are overdue with a blackmail payment." Aunt Agnes stopped speaking and looked at Joyce.

Of course, I knew that the note didn't mention blackmail—it simply mentioned an overdue payment. Clearly, Agnes was saying that in an attempt to trick Joyce. And it seemed to work.

Joyce hurried to the front door. At first, I thought she was going to escape, but she locked the door, flipped the sign to Closed, and pulled down the blinds. "Come into the back room," she said.

We followed her into a little office. She sat down at a desk and indicated we should sit too. There were no chairs opposite the desk, so Aunt Agnes and I pulled a chair each away from the chairs stacked against the wall. They were antique chairs and looked rather fragile, so I hoped they would take our weight. There was a laptop on the desk and a whole lot of papers, which Joyce cleared with one arm.

"Yes, Euphemia Jones and her husband, Ethelbert, were blackmailing me," she said in hushed tones. "Thankfully, the police never found out when they were investigating Ethelbert's murder."

"How long had they been blackmailing you, Joyce?" Agnes asked her.

"Not long-term," she said. "It all started when I had a Minton Lavabo in the shop. I was quite excited about it and I had decided to keep it for myself. Euphemia came in and wanted to buy it, but I said it wasn't for sale. She became quite angry, which I thought rather strange. Anyway, she must have done some digging into my past because she came back and said if I didn't give her the Lavabo, then she would make public the information she found out about me."

"What, let her have it for free?" I asked.

Joyce nodded.

"And what was the information, Joyce, if you don't mind me asking?" asked Agnes.

Joyce looked at Agnes and then put her head between her hands. "Years ago, when I was quite young and foolish, I received stolen goods and sold them on. It was years ago, mind you. I didn't have a dealer's licence at the time and I did it from home."

"Then how did Euphemia find out?" I asked her.

"I had a police record, of course," Joyce said. "I was charged."

"Did you have to go to prison?" Agnes asked her.

Joyce shook her head. "No, it was my first offence, but I had to do community service for a year. Plus, there was not much money involved, which helped my case."

"Then why were you worried if it became public knowledge?" I asked her.

"Because I'm an antique dealer and a rather successful one now," Joyce said. "If it got out that I had a criminal record for selling stolen goods, that could completely ruin my business." She drummed her fingers on the table. "And it's not just a business to me, you understand. It's my passion. Antiques are my passion."

"So, do you have any evidence that this was why she was blackmailing you?" Aunt Agnes asked her.

Joyce was visibly shocked. "No. Why?"

Aunt Agnes did not answer but instead asked, "And why were you late with the payment?"

"I'd sold a rare Chinese porcelain and panel floor screen, but the buyers had only left a deposit. They were coming to pick it up in person and pay the balance, but they were delayed because of bushfires in their region. They were regular customers and I expected them to be on time, so I told Euphemia she could have the money on that certain date. That was all."

"And she wasn't understanding?" Agnes asked.

Joyce narrowed her eyes. "She wasn't understanding about anything, that one. I'd rather deal with a Brown snake!"

Aunt Agnes stood up. "Thanks so much for confiding in us, Joyce. Of course, we won't breathe a word of it to anyone. I'm sorry Euphemia gave you such a hard time."

"I know she was your cousin, Agnes, but I'm not sorry she's dead," Joyce said. "That might sound harsh, but she was blackmailing me. I'm sure she was blackmailing plenty of other people as well."

Agnes patted Joyce on her shoulder. "I do understand. Well, I'm sorry I had to mention it, and I'll be in touch as soon as Jezabeth decides which antiques she wants."

Joyce nodded and showed us to the door. As soon as we were out of earshot, I turned to Aunt Agnes. "Did you believe her story?"

"I suppose so," Agnes said. "We do have the proof that she owed Gorgona money, but there could be more to it. I just don't know. Maybe, I'm just getting suspicious of everybody."

"Do you mean that you're worried Joyce could be working for The Other?" I asked her. "It's common knowledge that you love antiques."

"That's exactly what I was thinking," Agnes said as she threw her handbag in the back seat of her car.

CHAPTER 17

*A*unt Agnes looked up from her lemonade. "We need to question Karen Cosgrove."

We were sitting in the back garden under a big beach umbrella. Breena was sitting in the sand, hissing at Cary. She was in human form, and Aunt Agnes had told her to stay that way with Jezabeth being in such close proximity.

I kicked off my sandals and wiggled my toes in the sand. "I think that's going to be really difficult. Her lover would have already told her we'd been asking questions."

"It could make it easier," Dorothy said. "At any rate, you won't know until you try."

Maude picked up Cary. He had been rolling

199

and was covered with sand. "She might refuse to talk to us."

Agnes shrugged. "We don't have any other suspects and I'm confident it must be someone we already know."

"Do you still think it was a vampire?" Aunt Maude asked her.

Aunt Agnes tapped her chin for a while before answering. "I wouldn't say so categorically, but yes, I am leaning in that direction. It's what happened to Valkyrie that makes me think it must be a vampire."

"Because you think the intruder saw me at vampire speed?" I asked her.

She nodded slowly. "Yes, there's that but also the fact that they wanted to do away with you. An agent from The Other could possibly be angry enough to do that. If it was simply some normal person who had been blackmailed by Gorgona, then why would they want you dead too?" She shook her head. "No, the more I think about it, the more I think it could be a vampire."

"So does that mean we don't question Karen?" I asked her.

"No!" the aunts answered in unison.

"Karen could be a vampire," Aunt Dorothy pointed out.

"So could Joyce, but I don't really want to believe it," Agnes said. "I mean, it would be a bit of a coincidence if Gorgona was blackmailing someone who just happened to be a vampire in disguise as well."

"Maybe that's precisely what she was blackmailing Joyce about," I said to Aunt Agnes. "We only have Joyce's word that Gorgona was blackmailing her because of some youthful criminal convictions."

Aunt Agnes looked surprised. "You know, that hadn't occurred to me," she said. "But what would Joyce have against you? I mean, if she was working for The Other, then perhaps ..." Her voice trailed away and she shook her head. "Something doesn't add up. There is something I'm not seeing. I'm sure it will be obvious in hindsight, but for now, I'm not making the connection."

Aunt Maude put down her goblet of witches' brew and spread out her hands on the white iron garden table. "Let's look at the facts. We know somebody murdered Gorgona. We know Gorgona was blackmailing people. Now, what are the other motives for murder?"

"Love; money; revenge; wrong place, wrong time," I said. "There are probably others, but I can't think of them right now." I popped a small lemon meringue tart into my mouth.

"Well, I can't imagine Gorgona having a secret lover," Aunt Agnes said with a chuckle.

Maude disagreed. "It takes all types."

"There *is* the inheritance," I said. "What if Hemlock murdered her for the hundred thousand dollars? Goodness knows her drug habit would be expensive."

"It was one hundred and ten thousand dollars," Aunt Agnes corrected me.

I shrugged. "Or maybe Jezabeth murdered her to get her share of the inheritance. Perhaps Jezabeth lost her fortune."

"Have you seen all those designer clothes she wears?" asked Aunt Agnes.

"Maybe she's broke *because* of all her designer clothes," Maude said.

I reached over to stroke Cary. "And as for a wrong place, wrong time, motive, well, I suppose that's out of the question."

Aunt Maude nodded. "And then why did someone try to murder you, Valkyrie?"

"Maybe they thought I had seen them and could identify them," I said.

"Maybe." Aunt Maude took another sip of

witches' brew. "But for once, I agree with Agnes. I think there was malice directed at you, Valkyrie."

"You know, it's possible we have been looking at this all wrong," Aunt Agnes said. "Perhaps Gorgona was working for The Other, and either did a job for them badly, or refused to do it."

"You're not making any sense, Agnes," Aunt Dorothy complained.

Aunt Agnes gave a snort of disgust. "Okay, I wasn't explaining it well, but I meant to say that maybe The Other is responsible for Gorgona's death."

"But I shouldn't be in danger from The Other, surely? I mean, I know my parents are, but I shouldn't be, should I?" A trickle of apprehension ran up the back of my spine.

"No, otherwise, Lucas wouldn't have left you," Aunt Agnes said, scratching her head. "We are missing something here, but I don't know what it is. Breena, would you go into the kitchen and fetch us another bottle of witches' brew please?"

Breena nodded and glided off in the direction of the kitchen. She did walk like a cat, I thought as I watched her go.

"What if it was Breena?" Aunt Agnes said.

"Haven't you noticed how different she's been since Gorgona died?"

"Actually, she's been a lot more like a person and a lot less like a cat," I said. "I've noticed that."

"But what possible motive could she have?" Dorothy said. "Did she even know Gorgona?"

"Maybe Gorgona captured her and tortured her before she came to live at Mugwort Manor," Aunt Dorothy said. "Valkyrie said there was cat food in Gorgona's house."

"Plenty of people have cat food in their house, Dorothy." Aunt Agnes rolled her eyes.

"It *is* a bit of a stretch," Maude said.

Aunt Dorothy looked quite put out. "Seriously! What possible motive could Breena have had to murder Gorgona?"

Aunt Agnes looked behind her, but Breena hadn't emerged from the manor. "What if she *is* working for The Other? What if they put her here to spy on us in the first place?"

"But The Other hates shifters," I pointed out.

Aunt Agnes waved one finger in the air. "Breena is not an actual shifter, remember? There was a spell on her to make turn her into a cat. It's the spell that made her shift. Oh, here she comes now."

As Aunt Agnes changed the subject to Dorothy's

vegetables, I was left to wonder—what if Breena was the murderer? What if she had been working for The Other all this time? But why would she want to harm me? That didn't sit right with me. So then, if Breena had killed Gorgona, maybe it was somebody else who had tried to kill me? Aloud, I said, "Could there be two people involved in this?"

"Two people?" Aunt Agnes said in surprise.

"We've been assuming it was one person," I said with a slight nod of my head towards Breena, who was sitting in the sand swiping at passing ants, "but what if two people were involved? What if it was one person who murdered Gorgona and a second person who tried to murder me?"

Aunt Agnes frantically nodded and then said, "You might have something there, Valkyrie. But who could these two people be?"

"Karen Cosgrove and her lover, Franklyn Sutton," I said. "I could easily see the two of them working together. And what about Jezabeth and Hemlock? I could see them working together too. They might have murdered Gorgona to get the inheritance. Maybe Jezabeth is broke."

Aunt Agnes shook her head. "I already made some discreet inquiries and I know she's just as wealthy as she ever was. I actually wondered if she had murdered her mother to get the inheritance, so I did a bit of snooping."

"Then that's all the more reason we have to speak to Karen," I said.

Aunt Agnes agreed. "Let's go. We have already spoken to her lover and told him we're investigating Euphemia's death. I'll come straight out and ask Karen if she had anything to do with the murder."

I held up both hands, palms upwards, to the sky. "But what good will that do? She won't tell us the truth. She's hardly going to admit that she did it."

"Perhaps not, but we'll get a vibe from her," Aunt Agnes said. "Anyway, she's the last person left to question, so let's do it now and get it over with."

I checked the time on my phone. "Do we have time to question her before we show Linda the house?"

Aunt Agnes stood up. "We do if we go now. Breena, you had better come with us this time. I don't like leaving you alone at the manor. Or maybe you could stay with Dorothy?"

"No way, I'm coming too," Aunt Dorothy said.

"Okay Breena, you're coming with us. Don't speak to anyone, and if they speak to you, just nod at them," Aunt Agnes said. "I don't want to risk leaving you here alone in case the police come. And things seem to be getting more dangerous."

Soon the five of us were packed into Aunt Agnes's car, heading for Karen's manicure and pedicure salon.

Before long, we were standing outside the door. Aunt Agnes addressed us all. "I'll go in and ask her if she can come and have coffee with us now, but if she's in the middle of working on a client, we'll just have to wait."

Aunt Agnes was not gone for long. "Karen apparently has coffee by herself once a week at this time at a café on Main Beach," she said. "Let's all go there now."

"But who is she having coffee with?" I asked her.

"By herself. They said she goes every week to have time to herself," Agnes said.

"I wonder if she's meeting her lover there?" Maude asked.

"We will soon find out," Agnes said, "but I very much doubt they'd be seen together in such a public place. And Breena, don't drink anything out of a saucer."

"No, I won't," she said.

Breena really was saying more and more all the

time, and this had happened since Gorgona's death. That, to me, did seem significant, suspiciously so.

"How are we going to play this, Agnes?" asked Aunt Maude.

"Follow my lead."

Aunt Maude turned to her. "You really don't have any idea, do you?"

"No."

I thought this was going to be quite awkward. Still, I had no option but to follow Aunt Agnes into the café. Karen was indeed sitting alone, her back to the entrance, with a huge plate of scrumptious cupcakes in front of her.

"A party of five?" the enthusiastic waitress asked us. "Why don't you have that table over there? Would that suit?"

Aunt Agnes pointed to the table closer to us. "Is this one available?"

"Of course. Please sit down."

We all sat down and the waitress handed us menus. I kept my eye on Karen. She didn't turn around. We all ordered cupcakes and various types of tea. It was only after our cupcakes arrived that Agnes walked over to Karen. Karen jumped as she looked up at Agnes.

"Why don't you join us?" Agnes said.

Karen shook her head. I couldn't hear what she said, but Aunt Agnes apparently ignored her. "I insist!" Agnes said. "At least sit with us for one cupcake."

Karen turned around. Her eyes widened when she saw us all. "Just drag your chair over to our table," Agnes continued. "I'll buy you a cupcake. What sort would you like?"

"I couldn't eat any more," Karen said in a small voice once she sat at our table.

"Well then, there's no point beating about the bush," Aunt Agnes said. "By now, you would know we have spoken to you-know-who."

Karen's eyes widened and she nodded.

It only just occurred to me that Karen might want to kill me because I was responsible for her husband being in jail. On the other hand, maybe she was grateful to me for getting him out of the way.

"Did you know that somebody attacked Valkyrie? They hit her over the head, dragged her into one of our cottages, and set fire to it?"

Karen looked shocked at the news. To me, her shock was genuine. I continued to stare at her, trying to judge her reactions, as Aunt Agnes continued. "We think whoever murdered Euphemia Jones tried to murder Valkyrie."

Karen finally found her voice. "But are you sure your boarder was murdered? My friend told me the police said it was natural causes."

"They thought so at first," Aunt Agnes said, "but now they've discovered it was poison."

Once again, she looked shocked and once more, I judged her shock to be genuine. "Poison?" she repeated.

Aunt Agnes nodded. "I expect the police will be questioning you soon."

Karen was clearly thoroughly terrified. "But I didn't do it. I didn't poison anybody," she said. "It's my husband who's a murderer, not me!" She pulled a tissue out of her pocket and rubbed her eyes. When she took the tissue away, two big black circles surrounded her eyes. "I know my um, friend and I had a motive, but it wasn't us."

"I'm sorry to have upset you, Karen," Aunt Agnes said.

Karen stood up, picked up her handbag, and hurried away.

"What you make of that?" Aunt Agnes said.

"She did look genuinely shocked when you said

someone tried to murder me," I said. "I really don't think it's her. I don't think she was acting."

"Nor do I," Aunt Maude said.

"I didn't think she was acting either," Dorothy said.

Breena didn't say anything but continued to nibble on a lemon cheesecake cupcake.

"Maybe she looked shocked because something dawned on her and she knew it was her lover, after all," Agnes said.

Maude and Dorothy disagreed, while I suddenly noticed the time on my phone. "Horrors! We had better hurry. Linda will be at the house in ten minutes."

CHAPTER 18

"Sorry we're late," I said to Linda after I hopped out of Aunt Agnes's car outside Gorgona's house.

"No, you're right on time," Linda said. "This house looks even better in real life than it did on the Internet in street view."

Linda and I walked up the stairs. When I reached the top, I looked around to see why the aunts hadn't followed me. Aunt Agnes was trying to coax Breena out of the car.

"She's probably afraid of new places," Linda said. "I know she wasn't born as a shifter, but she would still have shifter characteristics even though she got them by means of a spell."

I was about to go back down and suggest Aunt

Dorothy or someone stay in the car with Breena, but she walked up the steps, looking around furtively. Her eyes were huge.

"It's okay," I said in soothing tones. "Maybe Aunt Dorothy could sit with you while the rest of us show Linda around the house."

Breena simply nodded.

"That's a good idea," Aunt Dorothy said, putting her arm around Breena's shoulders.

As soon as we walked inside, Hemlock appeared. "I thought it was only a real estate agent coming," she said by way of greeting. "What are you all doing here? Are youse allowed to be here?" She shot me a particularly spiteful look and then looked Breena up and down.

"The real estate agent is Linda who is a friend of mine. You met her at dinner the other night."

"And my sisters and I are executors of the will," Aunt Agnes said.

Hemlock pointed at Breena, who was still looking terrified. "And who is she?"

"She is my assistant," Linda said.

Aunt Agnes at once went on the offensive. "And what are you doing here, Hemlock? We specifically said you couldn't be here when there were any showings. We gave you plenty of notice."

"I lost track of time. I've just been down to the beach," she said in a petulant tone. "Now, how long will youse be here? I don't want to have to go out for long. I'm bored. There's nothing to do in this town."

"I'll text you as soon as we leave," Aunt Agnes said.

"I'm going to have to sage this house when I come back," Hemlock snapped. "Youse all give it bad energy." With that, she stomped out of the front door.

"We might as well start here in the living room," Aunt Agnes said.

Linda pointed to the antiques. "Can we get these antiques out of the way before it goes on sale? The place would look so much better if it's photographed without all these antiques."

Aunt Agnes readily agreed. "Yes, of course. There's plenty of time for that. We haven't even applied for probate yet—we have to wait for the death certificate to be sent to Jezabeth before we can apply. It will probably be months before we can list the house."

"If any clients ask about a house like this, I can certainly tell them it's coming up for sale," Linda said. "Wow, this house is massive. I knew it was big

MORGANA BEST

from the outside, but it's even bigger than I expected."

"It doesn't have much of a back yard, though," I told her. "Come and see." I led Linda out the back and showed her the back yard.

"No room for a pool," she said. "That will be a drawback as far as the price goes."

"Do people who live so close to the beach still want a pool?" I asked.

"Absolutely, especially houses in this upper price range! And besides, the Lighthouse Bay beach is shut today due to the shark warning. That happens a lot."

I looked up to the sky and saw the shark watch helicopter flying overhead. "Yes, I can see why someone would want a swimming pool, then," I said.

We walked back inside. "It has six bedrooms and three bathrooms," I said. "Hemlock is living in the master bedroom at the moment, but all the other bedrooms are free."

Aunt Agnes beckoned us over. She opened the door to the first bedroom and then let out a gasp. I hurried past her, half expecting to see a dead body, but I saw a pile of towels on the ground. They were soaking wet.

Aunt Agnes muttered a few rude words and picked them up. "These are beach towels! Hemlock must have dropped these when she came back from the beach."

"What was she doing in this room?" I said. "She's supposed to be restricted to the master bedroom."

Aunt Agnes hurried past me with the wet towels in the direction of the laundry room.

She let out another shriek. We all hurried to the laundry room. Once more, I half expected to find another body. To my relief, there wasn't one, but Aunt Agnes was pointing to a big sign taped over the washing machine.

It read,

> *'Dear Aunts, I hope youse aren't expecting*
> *me to pay for the water and electricity*
> *here. Obviously youse have to pay for it.*
> *I'm just a houseguest. Love and light*
> *from Hemlock. xxx'*

Linda turned to me, her jaw open. "Is she for real?"

I simply shrugged. "And it's all made worse by

the fact that she's a relative of mine," I said, rolling my eyes.

Aunt Dorothy and Breena had come to the laundry room at Aunt Agnes's second scream. "Well, we might as well take a tour of the rest of the house," Aunt Agnes said. "I can assure you, Linda, that this house is going to be shipshape by the time probate is through. We'll kick Hemlock out by then and we'll have the house professionally cleaned."

When we reached the kitchen, I was shocked to see mess everywhere. Open packets of food were scattered about, and dirty plates lined the kitchen sink.

"How long has Hemlock been living here?" Linda asked.

"Just a few days," I told her.

Linda made a clicking sound with her tongue. "This won't do at all. It smells foul."

I was about to say it didn't smell that bad when I remembered that Linda was a shifter wolf. Of course, everything would smell worse to her, given her heightened senses.

As we progressed through the bedrooms and bathrooms, it seemed as though Hemlock had left her mark on every room. "Does she have any friends in town?" Linda asked. "How can one girl make all this mess?"

"No idea," Aunt Agnes said with a sigh. "Now, the next room is the fifth bedroom. It's upstairs and has lovely views, but Gorgona was using it as an altar room."

Linda ground to a halt. "It will have wards against shifters."

Aunt Agnes patted her shoulder. "You don't need to worry. I cleansed it thoroughly, and it's perfectly safe now. It took some doing, I can tell you!"

Linda hesitated at the altar room door and then stepped inside. "That's a relief," she said. "I can't feel anything. You certainly did a good job in here."

Just then, we heard a scream behind us. I swung around, somewhat disoriented. For a minute, I thought Aunt Agnes had found something else Hemlock had done, but Aunt Agnes had been standing in front of me.

It was Breena. Her hands were clutching her face and her mouth was wide open. She turned around and ran down the stairs.

"What was all that about?" Aunt Dorothy asked.

"I don't know," Aunt Agnes said. "Well, don't

just stand there, Dorothy—get after her and find out what's wrong."

I crossed to the window and looked out. To my surprise, Breena ran out the front of the house. I hoped Dorothy would be behind her.

Jezabeth's car pulled up. "Didn't you tell Jezabeth that we were showing the house to a real estate agent?" I said to Aunt Agnes.

"No, I only told Hemlock," she said. "I don't know why that irritating girl didn't tell her mother."

To my horror, Jezabeth caught Breena by the arm and twisted it behind her back. She forced her into her car and drove off at speed.

CHAPTER 19

J swung around. "Jezabeth kidnapped Breena!"

I looked back out the window to see Aunt Dorothy standing on the street watching Jezabeth drive away at high speed. I turned to Aunt Agnes. "What are we going to do? Why would she kidnap Breena?"

"Maybe she thinks we're onto her. Maybe she murdered her mother, so she kidnapped Breena to use as a bargaining tool," Aunt Maude said.

"Or maybe she knows Breena is really a shifter cat," I said in fright.

"Oh my goodness!" Linda was looking at some of the potions in the cupboard. "Oh my goodness!" she said again.

Aunt Agnes went over to her. "We can't worry about anything now, Linda. We have to find Breena."

"I might be able to throw some light on that subject," Linda said.

"What you mean?" I asked. "Those herbs and potions could tell you where Jezabeth has taken Breena?"

"Not necessarily where, but I think I can tell you why."

By now Dorothy was back in the room. "Jezabeth took Breena against her will!" Her face was white.

"We know. I saw her out the window," I said, "but Linda has something to tell us."

"Can't it wait until later?" Dorothy said.

"Hush, Dorothy," Aunt Agnes said. "What is it, Linda?"

"These potions here—I've never actually seen them, I've only heard about them—are very strong, horribly potent potions."

"What are they used for?" Aunt Agnes said.

"They're used in a very dangerous and very rare ritual to turn somebody into a shifter."

"Are you saying Gorgona turned someone into a shifter?" Aunt Maude asked her.

Linda gestured to the cupboard. "All shifters know about this, but it's more of myth than anything because it's so rare. It's a way to turn someone into a shifter without biting them. Obviously, it's completely illegal."

"Is it permanent?" I asked her.

"Yes," Linda said, "and there's more."

Aunt Agnes waved one hand at her. "Then do tell us. We're running out of time to find Breena. Every moment counts."

Aunt Maude interrupted her. "If somebody can turn someone into a shifter like that, how come I've never heard of it?"

"You probably have heard of it but you've forgotten," Aunt Agnes said. "It does ring a bell with me, but I haven't heard of it for decades, maybe even longer."

Linda shook her head. "It's a terrible thing. It turns someone into a shifter, but it makes them the puppet of the person who turned them."

"What do you mean, a puppet?" I asked her.

"It means… um, okay, let me give you an example. Say I wanted to turn someone into a shifter by this method. After I performed the ritual, the person would be at my beck and call, and they would have to do whatever I said."

I was shocked. "Do you mean the person who did it could make the shifter murder for them?"

Linda bit her lip and thought for a moment. "No, nothing like that. I'd say it would be more like hypnosis, that it couldn't really make someone do things they wouldn't normally do. I've heard of it used for spying."

"How would it be any use for spying?" Aunt Maude asked her.

Linda turned one of the bottles around. "Well, imagine if you turned somebody into a cute puppy and gave the puppy to a family. The shifter puppy could report back everything about the family."

"But when did Breena have the opportunity to report to Gorgona?" I asked.

Aunt Agnes shrugged. "Maybe Gorgona hadn't wanted her to yet. Maybe she was only going to get reports from Breena every five years or so."

Linda nodded and continued to speak, explaining in more detail, but I was only half listening. Aloud, I said, "Gorgona turned Breena into a shifter cat and sent her to spy on you. Gorgona must have been working for The Other."

"But we didn't see anything in her house pertaining to The Other," Aunt Maude said.

I shook my head. "Jezabeth must have got in first and taken any incriminating evidence."

"But she said she didn't have a key," Agnes protested.

"Obviously, she was lying," I said. "Think about it. If Jezabeth wasn't working for The Other, then why would she kidnap Breena? And she and her mother didn't get on at all, and her mother didn't leave her as much in the will as you would expect. Still, it seems Jezabeth was protecting The Other, rather than her mother."

"Yes, what you say makes sense," Aunt Agnes said.

I pushed on. "That explains the cat food cans," I said. "And that explains why Jezabeth kept asking you whether we had a pet cat."

"So Breena was spying on us all this time!" Aunt Dorothy said. "I'm so upset."

"It was clearly against her will," I said. "Breena wouldn't harm any of us, and she did know about…" I caught myself before I blurted out about my parents and instead added, "about certain matters. We didn't want anyone else to know and she didn't tell anyone."

"Yes, you're right," Aunt Agnes said. "We can't speak of such things in this house, because it is not secure. Breena was certainly party to some things we need to keep private. Clearly, she is to be trusted."

"It also explains why Breena has started acting like a person to a rather large degree ever since Gorgona was murdered," I said. "Does that fit with what you know about these made shifters, Linda?"

Linda nodded. "Definitely. When the person who turns them dies, they regain their control and the spell is broken."

"But Breena still has cat mannerisms and acts like a cat from time to time," Aunt Maude protested. "And she's not speaking fully like a person yet."

"But that is to be understood," Linda said. "There's nothing supernatural about that at all. She lived as a cat for so long that it would be hard for her to adjust to being human. It's entirely natural."

I nodded slowly. "Yes, that makes sense. Now, where would Jezabeth take Breena?" Something occurred to me. Before anyone had a chance to respond, I added, "Can Breena still shift into a cat?"

Linda looked surprised. "Yes."

"But didn't you say the spell was broken?" Aunt Maude asked.

"Yes, but she's still a shifter. It's just that the spell forcing her to become a shifter has broken off her."

"I'm not sure I understand," Aunt Maude said.

Aunt Agnes sighed. "Honestly, Maude! It's quite clear."

"It isn't clear if I don't understand it," Maude protested.

Aunt Agnes held up one hand for silence. "What Linda means is that Breena is still a shifter. However, Gorgona no longer controls her. Gorgona forced Breena to become a cat against her will. It was only our spell that broke Gorgona's spell and allowed Breena to shift back into a human."

"That's right," Linda said.

Aunt Agnes continued. "However, Breena is now permanently a shifter and can turn into a cat at will. Still, I think it is clear that she was turned into a shifter cat initially against her will. Is that right, Linda?"

"Yes, you explained it well," Linda said.

"Should we be standing around here talking or should we be looking for Breena?" Maude said.

"Where do we start?" I said. "We don't know where Jezabeth would take her. Obviously, she hasn't taken her back to the cottage and she can't book a motel room and take her there, because someone would see Breena struggling."

"Maybe she's just going to drive around the bush and find somewhere private to force her to talk," Agnes said.

"But she doesn't know Breena can shift into a cat," I said.

They all looked at me. Aunt Agnes smiled. "Valkyrie, you're right!"

"Then could someone explain it to me?" Maude said more than a hint of disgust in her voice. She glared at Aunt Agnes.

Agnes nodded. "Sure. I doubt Jezabeth knows the circumstances of the spell. She wasn't close with her mother, and all her moves seem to be to help The Other. She knew her mother turned Breena into a cat, but I doubt she knows the intricacies of shifter spells. After all, *I* don't even know them and I'm much older than Jezabeth."

"*Much* older," Aunt Maude said with a snicker.

Aunt Agnes ignored her. "And Linda is the expert on this, and as we know, agents of The Other do not speak with shifters. No offence, Linda."

"None taken," Linda said. "We don't know how far away she'll take Breena before she turns into a shifter cat, and I'm assuming Breena doesn't have a phone?"

We all shook our heads.

"Then I assume Breena will turn into a cat at the first opportunity and make her way back to Mugwort Manor," Linda said. "We should all go there now and wait for Breena to turn up."

"We could always capture Hemlock and hold her for ransom—you know, make Jezabeth swap them," I said hopefully.

"I doubt Jezabeth will answer her phone to make such an arrangement," Agnes said.

"Then what do we do with Hemlock? What if she's working for The Other too?"

"We should take Hemlock back to the manor and keep an eye on her until we find out what Jezabeth is doing," Agnes said.

Just then we heard an angry voice yelling from downstairs. "What are youse still doing here?"

CHAPTER 20

e hurried down the stairs. I was at a loss as to what to do, but Aunt Agnes took charge. "Hemlock, your mother was just here looking for you. We're all having a big dinner tonight at the manor and she wants you to come with us now."

"I'll come later," Hemlock said. Her tone was belligerent.

"Your mother specifically asked you to come with us now," Agnes said. "She will meet you at the manor. She's got a surprise for you."

Hemlock's eyes narrowed. "What sort of a surprise?"

Aunt Agnes shrugged. "She didn't tell me. I'm just the messenger. Your mother asked me to take you back to Mugwort Manor because she is bringing a surprise for you. And then tonight, we are all having dinner together."

Hemlock pulled her phone out of her handbag and tapped away at the keys. "She's not answering," she said.

"No, because she's organising the surprise," Agnes said. "Okay then, you stay here if you don't want to come with us, but make sure you tell your mother that we gave you the message correctly."

"Oh, there's no need to make such a fuss," Hemlock said. "I'll come with youse. I just have to get something from my room." She hurried off into her room.

"Quick, grab her laptop," Aunt Agnes said to Linda. "It will fit in your briefcase."

Linda ran over to the coffee table in front of the huge television. Half-eaten cakes and packets of chips were strewn all over the table and scattered on the floor under it. Linda shut the laptop and shoved it into her briefcase. She had only just shut her briefcase when Hemlock came back. Luckily, Hemlock didn't look over in the direction of the coffee table.

"Okay, let's go." Agnes hurried everybody out the door.

When we reached the cars, Aunt Agnes said to Dorothy, "Why don't you go with Linda so there's room for Hemlock to come with us?"

Aunt Dorothy did as she asked, and soon we were all speeding to Mugwort Manor. I was terribly worried about Breena. What if Jezabeth had driven her away a fair distance before she had time to shift? Breena didn't have a phone, and I doubted she knew how to use one.

I hoped that Jezabeth had taken her to some isolated sand dunes close to the manor. After all, everyone was staying away from the beaches at the moment because of all the shark warnings.

I was glad Aunt Agnes had managed to get Hemlock to come with us peaceably. I was certain the girl would be a handful if she was forced to do something against her will.

Hemlock was chattering away about people she did not like, which turned out to be most of the world's population. She complained incessantly about everything. It only served to make me more stressed. When we got to the manor, I looked around for Breena in her cat form, but she was nowhere to be seen.

Aunt Agnes ushered Hemlock inside. I figured if it came to it, the aunts could overpower her and

lock her in the spelled crate in their altar room.
When I had first arrived in Mugwort Manor, they
had kept a rogue shifter trapped in there, so I knew
they would be able to imprison Hemlock without
any trouble.

I hadn't had a chance to ask the aunts if they
thought Hemlock was involved in any way with
Jezabeth in Gorgona's murder. Still, it was good that
we had her with us so we could keep a close eye
on her.

We all walked into the kitchen and Aunt Agnes
wasted no time pouring a glass of witches' brew for
everyone. "When is my mother coming?" Hemlock
asked Aunt Agnes.

"I have no idea," she said. "Why don't you try
calling her again?"

Hemlock did as she asked. "It's gone straight to
voicemail again," Hemlock said. "This surprise had
better be good."

"I'm sure it is a big surprise," Aunt Agnes said.
"Well, she could be another hour or so away. What
do you want to do in the meantime, Hemlock? Do
you want to watch Netflix or something?"

"I suppose. There's nothing else to do."

"Maude, you said you were keen to watch some
Netflix," Aunt Agnes said.

Aunt Maude looked up from fussing over Cary, who had just woken up. At first, she looked blank but then said, "Oh yes, I did. I'll go with Hemlock and we can find something to watch."

The two of them walked off, Hemlock looking none too pleased.

Moments later, there was a scratching sound at the back door. "Breena!" Agnes said. We both raced for the door, but Agnes beat me to it. She flung open the door.

There was a small black cat. She immediately morphed into a human. Aunt Agnes took off her coat and threw it around her.

I hugged Breena. "We've been terribly worried about you. Did Jezabeth hurt you?" I asked her.

"I'm remembering more now," Breena said, in what I was sure was the longest sentence she had uttered since she had been turned into a cat. "Gorgona tried to make me spy on all of you."

We all stood there with our mouths open, surprised that Breena had said so much.

Aunt Agnes came to her senses first. "Where's Jezabeth?"

Breena shook her head. "Don't know."

"Did she see you shift?" Aunt Agnes asked.

Breena shook her head. "No."

235

"Are you certain?"

Breena nodded.

"Did she try to make you talk? Did she ask you any questions?" Aunt Agnes said.

Breena shook her head. "She tied me up. Locked the car. She left. The car window was down this much." She showed us the dimension with her hands. "I got out the window."

I mentally filled in the gaps. When Jezabeth left, Breena must have shifted into a cat and then climbed through the gap in the car window.

"Oh dear, why didn't we think of that?" Aunt Agnes said.

Before anyone could ask her what she meant, she pushed on. "Jezabeth obviously came back here. She must have driven as close as she could to her cottage. She would have taken the back road to the beach and then cut across the sand dunes to the cottage to fetch her stuff. Of course, she would have done that! How silly of me. Obviously, once she got her hands on Breena, she intended to leave town."

She looked at Breena. "Were you near here? Did Jezabeth take the back road to the beach?"

Breena nodded.

"Then she will search for you," Aunt Agnes said. "Everyone, be on your guard."

"But what will she do?" I said. "She's outnumbered."

Aunt Agnes was silent.

"Why didn't she call Hemlock?" I asked them.

Aunt Agnes shrugged. "No idea. Maybe she thought we'd be with Hemlock and didn't want to tip us off. Who knows?"

"You think she intends to leave town without Hemlock?" I asked.

"Perhaps. And now we have another problem— what to do with Hemlock?"

My thoughts went to the inheritance. "Jezabeth won't be able to get the inheritance because she murdered Gorgona."

"She doesn't need anything from the inheritance," Aunt Agnes said. "She is a very wealthy woman already, as I keep saying. The inheritance would be just a pittance to her. Actually, now that I think about it, I very much doubt she will come here. Once she snatched Breena, she knew the game was up. I think Jezabeth will leave town as fast as possible." She turned to Breena. "Are you sure you're all right, dear?"

Breena nodded. "I'm cold and hungry."

"We can't risk you going upstairs to your room to get changed, because we don't want Hemlock to know you're here. Valkyrie, you and Breena are about the same size. Take her back to your cottage and get her some clothes and something to eat. Keep your eye out for Jezabeth, but I think you will be quite safe."

"Okay."

"And take Hemlock's laptop."

"When are you going to give it back to her?" I asked.

"I was about to ask you to copy all the files in it, just in case she *is* involved in it all with her mother. Just copy all the files; don't bother to look at them first. Do you have enough USBs?"

I nodded. "I think so. I have quite a few."

"Then when you copy all the files, bring the laptop back here."

I nodded and Linda handed me her briefcase. "Keep the laptop in here. That way if Hemlock comes out, she won't see it."

I took the briefcase from Linda. "Come on," I said to Breena as we ducked out the kitchen door.

Once I was outside, I realised the weather had cooled somewhat, although it was only mid-afternoon. A strong wind had sprung up, blowing leaves across our path. I let Breena into my cottage and gave her some of my clothes.

When she came out of my bedroom, I handed her a cup of tea. "Here, drink this. I put a lot of sugar in it," I said.

She thanked me and took her tea to the sofa, where she perched on it like a cat would. I opened Hemlock's laptop and then went to fetch my USBs.

"Gosh, she has a lot of files on her computer," I said to Breena, who simply nodded and continued to sip her tea. "Are you hungry?" I asked her.

She nodded again, so I looked in the fridge. "I have some chocolate cake?"

Breena seemed happy with that, so I took her over a slice. I went back to the laptop and spent the next few minutes copying files. "I don't have as many USBs as I thought I did," I said. "I'll have to go back and ask Aunt Agnes for some more."

"I'll get them," Breena said.

"Breena, I know it's a bit chilly out there, but would you mind going as a cat? I don't want you to go alone in case Jezabeth is hanging around and sees you. It wouldn't be safe."

Breena turned into a cat by way of response. "And bring Aunt Agnes with you when you bring the USBs back—don't come alone."

Breena meowed and slipped through the cat door at the back of the house.

I copied as many files as I could onto my remaining USB and then put all the USBs in a container. While I was waiting for Aunt Agnes and Breena to return, I flipped through Hemlock's mail. She seemed to have a lot of emails with someone I suspected was her drug dealer, and she had plenty of eBay purchases. I idly flipped through those, but one brought me up short.

"Castor beans!" I exclaimed aloud. "Twenty-nine dollars? You can buy half a kilogram of castor beans for twenty-nine dollars, and it's legal to sell them?" I scratched my head and peered at the screen. Sure enough, Hemlock had bought a bag of castor beans on eBay.

So Hemlock was the killer, after all?

But why? I ran through the facts. She was a horrible person. I knew she didn't have a job. Could the motive have been financial? I figured it must have been. Hemlock had thought she was going to get even more in the will than the one hundred and ten thousand dollars that her grandmother had left her. Her mother had stopped giving her money. She had expensive tastes and appeared to be an addict. The more I thought about it, the more I figured that money was the motive.

I reached for my phone to call Aunt Agnes

when the door opened a crack. "Aunt Agnes," I said. "You'll never guess who the murderer is!"

The door opened wide. Hemlock was standing there. "I have a good idea," she said. She was holding a big knife.

I jumped to my feet and moved to my right, keeping the kitchen table between us. I looked around the room for something to use as a weapon. I knew Breena would bring Aunt Agnes back at any minute, so I had to keep Hemlock talking.

"You think you're so smart, but you didn't know it was me," she said with smug satisfaction.

"No, we didn't suspect you at all," I admitted. "What was your motive? Didn't you like your grandmother?"

"I liked her fine," Hemlock said. "She was nicer than my mother, but my mother isn't going to leave me anything in her will, and Grannie said she was going to leave me a lot. She was lying…" Her voice trailed away, but not before she called Gorgona some very fancy words. "And you didn't even check my alibi! I flew in from Adelaide a few days before you thought I did."

That surprised me. "So, you murdered your grandmother for her inheritance, nothing else?"

She looked surprised. "Why else would I murder her?"

"And how did you know about castor beans?"

A superior look crossed her face. "It was on one of my favourite TV shows. Someone had a castor oil plant growing in their garden and they took some beans off it and made poison to kill someone. I couldn't figure out the instructions online, but I read that if someone chewed a lot of beans, they would die and you know how much Grannie liked coffee!" She chuckled. "Anyway, I replaced most of Grannie's coffee in her grinder with castor beans. When they're ground, they're poisonous, you see."

I nodded, keeping my eye on the knife.

She glared at me. "How did you know it was castor beans?"

"I stepped on one when I saw you in the cottage that night. It was you, wasn't it?"

"Who else would it have been? Of course, it was me."

"I thought it might have been your mother."

"My mother? What would she be doing out after dark?

"Does your mother know you murdered Gorgona?"

"Honestly, you're stupid. Of course, she doesn't

know. Why would she know? Sometimes you say stupid things."

She advanced on me, holding the knife high. Where was Aunt Agnes? She sure was taking her sweet time. I had to keep Hemlock talking.

"So why did you try to burn me in the cottage that night?

"I don't like you," Hemlock said. "You're stupid."

"And you don't have a very large vocabulary," I countered.

"What you mean by that?" Hemlock looked confused.

I took the opportunity to look around the room once more for a weapon. Over the kitchen table was a freestanding lamp. Although I had an office in my cottage, I often sat at the kitchen table, and as the lighting there was poor, I used the freestanding lamp. It was metal. I jumped up and grabbed it.

Hemlock looked surprised. I don't think it occurred to her that I'd fight back.

She ran at me, the knife held high. She struck at me. I think she had been imbibing too many illegal substances because her aim was bad.

I brought the freestanding lamp down hard on her arm, causing the knife to fly from her grasp. Just then, Aunt Agnes burst through the door. Breena was in human form and wearing a bathrobe.

"Hemlock is the murderer!" I exclaimed. I pushed Hemlock to the ground and pinned her arms behind her back. "Why did you take so long?"

"I couldn't find USBs anywhere. While I was looking, Dorothy went to check on them and found Maude was fast asleep and Hemlock wasn't there," Aunt Agnes told me.

"Hemlock said Jezabeth didn't know she was the one who murdered Gorgona," I told them. "She did it for the inheritance."

"And youse didn't suspect me," Hemlock said. "I fooled youse all."

"Tell it to the Cleaner," Aunt Agnes said, pulling Hemlock to her feet.

A look of pure fear passed across Hemlock's face.

CHAPTER 21

"*I* just don't see why he gets to pee in the garden and I don't," Breena said as she scratched behind her ear. She was looking at Cary, the Dachshund, as he did his business beneath a flower bush.

"He's a puppy, Breena," I said. It was the fifth time I was having this conversation with Breena. Not that I minded. I am sure many people had to explain to drunken uncles who hadn't once been cats that peeing in the garden was unacceptable.

But Breena didn't seem to hear. "He's not even related to you and he gets all this special treatment."

I exhaled sharply. "Fine. If you like, you can

245

sneak out here after dark and tinkle on the roses then."

"You absolutely cannot," Aunt Agnes said stiffly. "They are my roses, and if anyone is going to tinkle on them, it will be me."

"No one is tinkling on any roses," Aunt Maude replied.

"Not unless you're a puppy," Breena muttered bitterly.

"Exactly. If you somehow get turned into a puppy by an evil vampire-witch next time, then you can pee in the garden," Aunt Dorothy said.

Breena did not seem totally content with this, but she lapped her lemonade from her glass.

I reclined in the chair, rubbing my temples. It was a little cool in the garden, twilight gathering around us with the moths and mosquitoes. I hardly wanted to think about the case I had just solved, since it had given me a crashing headache, so I felt a warm rush of relief when Cary padded over and started to lick my ankles.

"Stop it," I said, trying to shoo away the Dachshund when his licks turned to little nips, but that only seemed to make him more determined. "My ankles are not that interesting, Cary."

"I beg to differ," said a voice.

I whipped around. "Lucas!"

Laughing, I sprang from my chair and tossed myself into his arms, relaxing as I caught a familiar whiff of cinnamon and sandalwood, the cologne Lucas liked to wear. I felt the warmth of his hands through my thin cotton top, and I grinned.

"I'm gone for two seconds and you find yourself in mortal danger. I can never leave again."

"To be fair," I replied as Lucas released me from his strong grip, "I often find myself in mortal danger when you are around, too."

"Err, why is Breena squatting over there by the rose bushes?" Lucas replied, scratching his head.

"No!" Aunt Maude cried. She jumped to her feet, knocking over the garden table and scaring Cary.

"She has decided that if the puppy gets to pee in the bushes then so does she," I explained, slightly embarrassed. But if Lucas didn't realise my family was a bit kooky by now, then there really was no hope for our relationship.

"Seems reasonable," Lucas replied. He wrapped an arm around my shoulders. "Want to go for a walk along the beach?"

"Yes," I cried a little too loudly.

"Take Cary," Aunt Maude said, handing Lucas

the puppy's leash. "I think Breena is a little jealous of him."

Ten minutes later, Lucas and I found ourselves walking barefoot along the sand, the slight evening breeze occasionally whipping the hair out of my eyes. Now that Lucas was home, I felt as though I could breathe again, truly breathe, like I did when I was a child, riding a bike down the lane. It wasn't the calm sort of breathing celebrities talked about on late night talk shows, the type of breathing that quietened all the questions running through their heads. It was the kind of breathing that was accompanied by a swoop in the stomach and the prickle of nervous anticipation on the skin. The type of breathing suggesting that something big was coming and you better hold on for the ride, kid.

I wiped the sand out of my eyes, taking great pains to avoid my carefully applied eyeliner. When I got home, I would have a cat woman who wanted to pee on the roses, an aunt who refused to wear her glasses, and another two aunts who were bigger handfuls than a couple of toddlers. But for now, I had the beach and the twilight and the man I loved walking by my side.

It was stressful being a modern woman. On top of worrying about gut health, celery juice, probiotics, crystal infused water, organic produce, and climate change, I also had to worry about murder. I bet Gwyneth Paltrow never had a distant relative turned into a cat in order to spy on the family. Or maybe she did. Hollywood was, after all, a weird place.

"What are you thinking about?" Lucas said as he held me close.

"I'm glad you're back," I said, and my stomach twisted. I hadn't experienced butterflies like this since I was a teenager.

"I'm glad I'm back too," Lucas replied, as our lips met.

ABOUT MORGANA BEST

USA Today bestselling author Morgana Best survived a childhood of deadly spiders and venomous snakes in the Australian outback. Morgana Best writes cozy mysteries and enjoys thinking of delightful new ways to murder her victims.

www.morganabest.com

Made in United States
Orlando, FL
10 April 2022

16670720R00157